"Relax a bit, Mr. Kearns."

"He hates having his picture taken," Jess supplied.

"Oh, do I need to tell you how pretty you are?"

Wayne's eyebrows shot up in shocked surprise.

Not funny! Dena chastised herself as she went behind her camera to refocus. *I can't believe I said that.* She wished she had an old Cirkut camera so she could drape its dark cloth over her head and hide.

Wayne crossed his arms.

Great. Real professional, Dena. "Okay, where are those smiles I saw earlier?" Dena coaxed.

Jess massaged Wayne's shoulders.

He reached up and patted Jess's hands, splashing a grin across his face that could charm any woman. "I'm doing this for you, honey."

Lord, help me, I'm attracted to a married man. She glanced down at his ring finger. Nothing. She glanced up at Jess's. A small silver band encircled it. *He didn't buy her gold? Who is this guy?*

"Thanks, Dad." Jess kissed the top of his head.

"Dad?" The word tumbled from Dena's lips before she could stop it. Heat warm enough to be a hot flash rose across her cheeks. But this had nothing to do with hormones.

Or did it?

LYNN A. COLEMAN was raised on Martha's Vineyard and now calls Florida home. She has three grown children and eight grandchildren. She is a minister's wife who writes to the Lord's glory. She served as advisor of the American Christian Romance Writers, Inc. Lynn enjoys hearing from her readers. Visit her Web page at www.lynncoleman.com.

Books by Lynn A. Coleman

HEARTSONG PRESENTS

Photo Op

Lynn A. Coleman

Heartsong Presents

I'd like to dedicate this book to my loving husband, Paul, who is my constant encourager, lover, and friend. Thank you for all the hard work you put in on my behalf to help each project be the best it can be.

A note from the Author:
I love to hear from my readers! You may correspond with me by writing:

Lynn A. Coleman
Author Relations
PO Box 721
Uhrichsville, OH 44683

ISBN 978-1-59789-585-9

PHOTO OP

Our mission is to publish and distribute inspirational products offering exceptional value and biblical encouragement to the masses.

PRINTED IN THE U.S.A.

one

Dena glanced into the rearview mirror and touched up her lipstick. Grabbing her fully loaded cameras and backpack from the passenger seat, she ran into the church.

"Hey, Mom, didn't think you were going to make it." Jason wiped his hands on a semi-white apron. "Get in late last night?" He kissed her cheek.

Dena returned the affection and stepped back. "Yeah, I was busy developing some pictures and lost track of time." She glanced at her wristwatch. "I'm not that late."

"No problem. Your booth is outside. The teens set up a few lobster pots and buoys. I think they did a real good job. But you'll probably want to rearrange things."

"Probably." Dena chuckled.

Jason knew her all too well. She had been a professional photographer since he was a teen, and he had seen her work many photo shoots. Asking her to donate a full day of work wasn't too unusual. She'd do anything for her son. Plus, the money raised would help support the youth ministries at Jason's newest pastorate.

Billy and Susie ran into the church kitchen. "Grandma!"

Dena's joy spread from her heart to her open arms. She knelt to meet them. Billy, eight, thrust his arms around her. Five-year-old Susie followed with equal enthusiasm, and Dena reached down to catch herself from landing on her backside. "How are Grandma's little ones this morning?"

"Okay." Billy kissed her on the cheek. "There's so many booths, Grandma. And lots of food." *Any more enthusiasm and I'd need to wear earplugs.*

Dena stood up, straddling Susie on her hip. "And what about you, pumpkin?"

5

"I so 'cited. Daddy got a cotton candy machine." Susie's toothless grin widened. A natural blond with curly hair, the child reminded her of Jason when he was little. But thankfully, Susie had more feminine features, too—like her mother's nose and chin.

Susie wiggled down and ran off with her brother.

"Don't eat too much and get a tummy ache," Dena warned.

"We won't," the children said in unison.

"You're going to have your hands full tonight." She winked at Jason.

"Loaded up on the antacids yesterday. The kids don't know it, but there are corn dogs and french fries, along with the traditional Maine lobster and clam dinner this evening."

"I think I brought enough film." Dena tapped her large camera case. "Plus, I have my digital."

"Great. If you don't mind, could you get some candid digital shots just for the church? Maybe the Web page? How's the new digital SLR camera you bought yourself for Christmas?"

Dena grinned. "The learning curve has taken a bit longer than I'd hoped, but I'm getting the hang of it. I'll use the F2 for the professional shots." She pulled her old Nikon F2 SLR 35 mm camera out of the camera bag and placed it around her neck. In another month she hoped to be comfortable with digital. There were definite advantages to film. When out in the wilds, she didn't have to charge batteries or bring a laptop computer. What her son didn't know was that she now had two digital SLRs and a half dozen automatic lenses to go with them. She held up Old Faithful. "I can control the shot more with this one."

"Whatever, Mom. You're the pro."

Dena noticed the pies lined on the counter. "Need a hand bringing these out?"

"Sure." Jason balanced six pies on a large tray.

Dena scooped up two, one in each hand. "Lead on."

He pushed through the swinging doors with his back and stepped into the fellowship hall. Dena caught the door with her foot and kicked it open again, wiggling through the doorway, deftly holding the cream-covered pies.

They crossed the fellowship hall, weaving past tables, workers, and a few children running around. It smelled of wood, floor wax, and a slight musty odor. The pie table stood in close proximity to the front door. "Ah," Dena said, "getting them as they're leaving after tempting them when they walk in, huh?"

Jason's crooked grin hiked up his face. "Something like that." He placed his tray on the corner of an already full table and began making room for his six pies. Dena examined the area and decided to put the pies on the other end.

"I think we brought too many out," Jason offered.

"Do you have any crates we could stick under the table to place these pies on?"

"Jason, what are you doing?" Marie, Jason's wife, placed her hands on her hips. "Those are the pies for the pie-eating contest, not to sell. Didn't you notice the extra whipped cream on them?"

"Ahh, no. Sorry." He began placing the pies he'd put on the table back on his tray. "Guess you might as well bring those back to the kitchen, Mom."

"Sure." She chuckled. Some things never changed. Jason had been in the ministry for six years, and this was his second church. He was great at preaching, teaching, and caring for the members of his congregation. But little things, like where this went or that, always seemed to elude him. Thankfully, the Lord had blessed him with a wife who was gifted in the areas where he was lacking.

Dena turned sideways and pushed the door open with her shoulder, swinging her body forward as the doors opened. A little one ran under her arms. Dena lifted the pies, keeping them safe. "Kids," she muttered.

She turned toward the child. "Better slow down, sport."

The door banged into her arm and knocked it backward.

Shocked, she stood paralyzed as whipped cream and chocolate

pudding slowly oozed down her face.

"I'm so sorry." A handsome man with rugged shoulders and sandy blond hair stood in front of her holding a wire bushel basket full of lobsters. "Can I help you?"

"No," she stammered.

"Mom, are you all right?" Marie came running up to her side.

"Grab the camera. Unhook the strap. Get it off of me before the cream and pudding can work their way down on top of it."

"Sure." Marie fumbled with the strap and removed the camera.

"I'm sorry," the stranger apologized again.

Dena wiped the cream from her eyes. The one-man demolition crew placed his basket of lobsters on the floor. "Let me give you a hand."

"No, thanks, I'll just go to the parsonage and wash up." She turned and faced her daughter-in-law. "Marie, can you lend me a blouse?"

"Sure, Mom. Let's get some of the mess off of you first." Dena followed Marie the rest of the way into the kitchen.

The stranger stood there, aghast. *He might be a klutz, but he sure is a handsome one.* Dena stopped in midstride. Since when did she notice the opposite sex? Having been a widow for the past twenty years, dating was something she'd given up on long ago. At first she'd been emotionally raw from losing Bill. After that, she was too busy providing for herself and the children. She hadn't had time.

"Here, use this." Marie offered a handful of paper towels.

"Now I'm really running late."

"Don't worry about it, Mom. The photo booth is only open when you're there."

Dena scooped mounds of whipped cream and chocolate of her white cotton blouse. "Do you have any spot remover a home? I'd like to get some on this blouse before the chocolat sets."

"Of course. With Billy and Susie, I'd be crazy not to hav some on hand."

"Or with me." Dena chuckled. "I can't believe I didn't look."

"Well, there aren't any windows in those doors, so even if you had, you wouldn't have seen Wayne coming."

She never pictured a "Wayne" as being a rugged, outdoors type, but the name agreed with him. Of course, John Wayne fit that bill, but that was his last name. Actually, she recalled it wasn't even his real name. "I take it he was bringing in the lobsters for tonight's dinner."

"Yeah." Marie led the way to the back alley that would bring them to the rear door of the parsonage. The church and parsonage sat kitty-corner to each other, with a parking lot in the rear of the two buildings.

The parsonage was an old Victorian-style home with a large front porch. Inside, the hardwood floors showed years of use, but, with a little tender loving care, Dena was certain they could be restored. Many things needed fixing in the old place, and slowly Jason and Marie were getting them done. The congregation could afford it, but the previous pastor hadn't expressed concern about the condition of the house. The church members had remodeled the kitchen with all new appliances before Jason and his family arrived.

They stepped into the master bedroom. Marie pointed to the bathroom and then walked over to the closet.

"What about this one?" Marie pulled out a drop-collar white blouse with tiny teardrop roses in a pale pink.

"That'll be fine, thanks. Do you mind if I take a shower first? I feel kinda sticky."

"No problem." Marie pulled some clean towels from the closet and handed them to Dena. "Here ya go. Unless you need something else, I'm going to go back. There's no telling what that son of yours will mix up next."

"Sorry, he's your husband now." Dena waved off her daughter-in-law. "His shortcomings aren't my responsibility anymore."

"Thanks a bunch." Marie chuckled and exited.

❧

"I'm so sorry, Reverend. I didn't mean to bang into your mother. That was your mother, right?"

A low rumble escaped Pastor Russell's lips. "Yeah, that was my mom."

"It was kinda hard to tell. Not that I've ever seen her before. But I heard she was coming to town, and Mrs. Russell called her 'Mom,' so I just kinda put two and two together." He was rambling. He felt like a fool. The poor woman was literally creamed by those pies. Wayne fought to keep a smirk from surfacing as he pictured the cream sliding down her face and hanging from her chin.

"She'll be fine, Wayne." The pastor leaned over the basket of lobsters. "They all safe?"

Wayne looked down at the thick blue elastics used to keep the lobsters' powerful claws shut. "Yup. Wouldn't want someone losing a finger while putting them on the grill or in the pot."

Jason pulled his hand out of the basket.

Wayne snickered. "Landlubber."

"Hey, I'm learning. At least I don't expect live ones to be red anymore."

Wayne rolled his eyes. "Good. Look, Pastor Russell, I can't stay. I'm glad to lend a hand in any way I can, but I'm afraid I have a job I must complete today."

"That's fine, Wayne. Donating the lobsters is a tremendous gift."

"Wish I could have gotten more, but that's all I was able to pull out of my pots this week."

"It's a fine catch, thank you." Wayne took the pastor's extended hand. For a landlubber, he was all right. Pastor Jason's first year with the church had gone very well. People were excited about their church and enjoyed challenging themselves in their walk with the Lord. The small community of Squabbin Bay seemed just the right fit for Pastor Russell and his family. Wayne noticed he'd become more careful to give God His due in prayer, praises, money, and just plain old acknowledgment of who God is.

"I'll try and come back as soon as possible," Wayne offered.

"If you can't make it, I'll understand. Lord's blessings on your day, Wayne."

"Thanks, Pastor. Same to you."

He thought of mentioning that Jess was coming in today so they could have their picture taken, but now didn't seem like the right time to bring it up. Leaving the church, he slipped into the cab of his old pickup truck. He turned the key and the engine purred to life. The truck didn't look like much, but it ran well. A man didn't need a whole lot more.

As he pulled out of the parking lot, the image of the cream-covered woman replayed, and he finally surrendered. Wayne laughed so hard, tears edged his eyelids. The killer was when she wiped the cream off her eyes. He knew she was fighting giving him a piece of her mind. Her hands showed she was older than the rest of her appeared. Of course, she had to be older than he was to be the mother of Pastor Russell. He tried to imagine her with Jason's face. Wayne shuddered. *Nope, won't go there.* He pulled up to the house where he was building some new cabinets, grabbed his toolbox from the bed of the truck, and proceeded inside.

Henry Drake was in his eighties and liked work done well. He'd watch over Wayne's shoulder constantly. At first Wayne found it quite annoying. But when he learned that Henry was a combination of lonely and curious, he soon appreciated him hanging around.

"Morning, Henry. Sorry I'm late."

"Heard you creamed the pastor's mother."

Wayne groaned.

two

Wayne hoisted his toolbox into the back end of the pickup, then rolled his shoulders and stretched. His cell phone rang as he slipped into the cab, requiring awkward contortions to retrieve it. "Hello."

"Hey, Dad, I'm at the church fair. Where are you?"

"Just finished up Henry Drake's job. I've got to run home for a shower. And I'll meet you there."

"No problem. Remember, you promised to take a picture with me."

"How could I forget?" Wayne turned the key and headed toward his place. "So, did you bring the mystery man with you?"

"Daaaad!" Jess dragged his name out long enough that he could hear the laughter in her voice.

"Well, did ya?" he sang back.

"Trev promised he'll visit next time."

Third time. The kid doesn't want to meet me. I don't like it, Lord. "Well, I'm looking forward to meeting him."

"You will like him, Dad, I promise."

"I'm sorry for you that he couldn't make it this weekend, honey."

"I love him, Daddy. He's a good man. He works hard, just like you."

Wayne felt a slight grin rise on his right cheek. He'd worked hard for the past twenty-two years. Jess was in her senior year of college and seriously considering marriage. Life was changing, and perhaps a bit too fast. He wasn't sure.

"I love ya, Jess, and I trust you." He let out a slow breath. It wasn't easy trusting your daughter to the dangers of the world. Especially knowing she came into this world because of a mistake he'd made with her mother when he was seventeen years old.

"Thanks, Daddy. I love you, too. Don't forget to dress for the picture. I've seen some of the photographs the pastor's mother has done; they're awesome. She ought to be a professional."

"She is. Pastor Jason says she travels the world."

"Wow. Maybe I should switch majors."

"If you do, you'll pay for it. I've paid for one college education. I won't be paying for a second."

Jess laughed. "Gotcha."

"I'll be there in half an hour, forty minutes tops."

"Okay, later."

The phone went dead before he could respond. Four years, and it still bothered him that she was growing up and would one day be totally on her own. She'd been his life. He'd worked overtime to bring in the monies needed. Jessica's mother had quickly agreed to his raising her. It had been an easy arrangement. Terry didn't want a child, and at sixteen she'd had a lot of growing up yet to do. The first year they'd flirted with the idea of getting married and becoming a real family after she got out of high school. They soon realized they had nothing more than a physical attraction between them. Terry had signed full custody over to Wayne, and for a while she visited Jess. After a couple years, college, a new city, and eventually her own family, Terry did little more than write an occasional letter.

Lord, please don't let the sins of the father be passed down to the daughter. His silent prayer for twenty years now, since he'd accepted Jesus as his personal Lord and Savior, remained as fervent as ever. If ever anyone understood the grace of God taking mistakes and turning them into blessings, he certainly did. Jessica was his pride and joy. He just wasn't ready to see her completely out of his life.

❧

The churchyard bustled with people. "Hey, Wayne." John

Dixon waved. "How's it goin'?"

Wayne shook John's beefy hand. "Fine, fine. How 'bout yourself?"

"Couldn't be better. The wife's fixing to have quite a vegetable garden this year."

"Zucchini?" Wayne couldn't help but wonder how they would get rid of all the zucchini this year. Last year they'd brought it in bushel baskets to the church. Most folks had enough of the vegetable from their own gardens. A couple boys took a basket full and used it for target practice.

John's grin slipped as he looped his thumbs behind his red suspenders. John and Rita were in their sixties, and the garden grew each year as John put out fewer lobster pots. "I've got her planting half as many of those. This year I expect to have a bumper crop of pumpkins. Now a man can make a profit from those."

"Rita sure has a green thumb." Wayne scanned the crowd, looking for his daughter.

"Jessica?" John asked.

"Yeah, have you seen her?"

"Saw her over by the dunk tank. Pastor Jason was taking quite a drenching."

Wayne was glad he'd dressed in his fisherman's sweater. He wouldn't be taking a dip in the tank today. "Did you have a hand in dunking him?"

"Well, maybe once." John looked from side to side. "I adjusted the sensitivity so high, you can practically blow on it and it will dunk the man."

"John, is that any way to treat the pastor?"

John winked. "Why not? It's for charity."

"I might just go and rescue the man by readjusting your adjustment."

"Don't bother. Dennis Cowen already figured it out and fixed it."

"Wise man."

"Spoilsport is what I say." John chuckled at his own humor.

"I take it it's your turn next in the dunking pool?" Wayne suggested.

"Now what would be the fun in seeing an old man getting dunked?"

"Plenty, especially if the pastor is the first to take a shot at ya."

John roared. "I'll fess up later, after dinner."

"You do that." Wayne winked. "Well, I've got to find Jess. I promised her we'd have our picture taken."

"Heard you creamed the pastor's mother earlier."

Wayne felt the back of his neck get as red as a boiled lobster. "It was an accident."

"Seems a handyman like yourself might find the time to put some windows in those doors so others won't run into the same fate," John suggested.

"Already thought of it. Finding the time will be the problem."

"I hear ya." John looked past Wayne's shoulder. "I've got to find Rita. I'm looking forward to dinner and want to get our seats."

"Later." Wayne waved and walked toward the events area before John came up with something else to chat about. He was a nice guy and all, but John knew how to bend a man's ear.

Wayne waved at Billy Hawkins, who was leading his old paint horse around the church's perimeter, giving pony rides. It carried a young girl in blond hair and pigtails whose smile showed a mixture of joy and fear. He moved farther back toward the dunking pool where a gang of people had gathered around one shriveled-up pastor. His blue lips proved he'd been dunked one too many times. "Better dry off, Pastor." When Wayne was the youth director, he'd seen the inside of the tank one too many times.

Pastor Jason smiled. "I see you aren't risking it."

"No, sir. I promised Jessica a picture."

He shivered. "Ah, good plan."

His wife, Marie, came up beside him with an oversized towel and wrapped him up. They were an interesting couple. They appeared very content with their relationship, and that's what mattered most, Wayne reckoned.

"Daddy!"

He turned in the direction of his daughter's voice. She held up a cream pie and pointed at him. Across the table was Jess's best friend from high school, Randi. "Don't you dare. You said you wanted this picture."

She placed the pie back on the bake sale table and scooted up beside him. "Had to tease you. Everyone's talking about how you creamed the pastor's mother. Nearly ruined her favorite camera, too." She leaned back and called out to Randi, "Call me?"

"All right." Randi waved and headed in the opposite direction.

Wayne cupped his hand over the one Jess placed in the crook of his elbow. "Perhaps we better not bother Mrs. Russell."

"Afraid she has a pie waiting for you?"

"Since when did you become a wicked woman?" he teased. Playful banter had been a part of his and Jess's relationship ever since she was five.

"Learned it from a master." She kissed his cheek.

They strolled toward the photo booth. "It's good to see you. How are your final papers coming?"

"I've got a serious case of senioritis."

"How so?"

"I can't concentrate. Thank the Lord I'm managing somehow. But Dr. Wilson is probably longing for this class of seniors to graduate. Soon."

Wayne wrapped her in his arms. "Like you said, it's senioritis. And while I didn't go to college, I do recall my senior year in high school."

"Me, too. This is worse. Big time."

He kissed the top of her head. "You'll get through it. I love you, princess."

She leaned up and kissed him again. "I love you, too."

They stopped at the small table to register for their photo. Misty Williams, a gal who was in the junior high youth group he'd led a few years ago, smiled and blew a pink bubble that nearly covered her face. "Hey ya, Mr. Kearns, want your picture taken?"

❧

Dena spotted Wayne Kearns through her digital camera's 300mm zoom lens long before he saw her. He was wrapped in the arms of a girl half his age. *He could be her father!* she wanted to scream. Observing them a bit longer than necessary, Dena saw they truly loved each other. *Forgive me, Lord. Who am I to say who should and shouldn't be together? Jason spoke highly of Wayne and cherished his ministry with the church.* After taking a few pictures of the couple, she lowered the camera. It was the only way to get some candid shots in between the portrait pictures.

"Mommy, I don't want my picture taken."

She knelt down to the five- possibly six-year-old girl with reddish brown hair. Dena rolled her shoulders and fired off a prayer. At fifty-two, there were many reasons she no longer did studio work—and dealing with testy children was one of them. But for Jason and the Lord, she could endure anything. "What's a pretty little girl like you doing here?"

The young child scrunched up her face.

Dena mimicked the girl. "You don't have to have your picture taken, but it would be a shame if the church directory didn't have a picture of such a pretty seven-year-old."

"I'm five," she corrected, and a smile lifted the corners of her lips.

"My, my. You definitely look mature. A fine young lady if ever I saw one."

"Really?"

"Really." Dena extended her hand to shake the child's. "Sorry I can't take your picture, but it was a pleasure meeting you."

Hesitantly, the freckled girl extended her hand. "You can take my picture, if you'd like."

"Why, thank you, Miss. . . . What is your name?"

"Clarissa."

"Clarissa. A pretty name to go with a pretty face. Come, sit right here and I'll take your picture. Then you can go back to the church fair and play the games. What's your favorite game, Clarissa?" Dena adjusted the camera on the tripod and changed the f-stop for the now-glowing child. In her hand Dena held the remote attached to the camera. She smiled. In the eighties, when she'd purchased the cable release, it was state-of-the-art. Today it seemed old-fashioned—a simple cable with a piston and a push button on the end.

"I like the ring toss. I got a teddy bear."

Click. Dena fired off a fast round of several frames. "Wow, you must be really good. I've never managed to get a ring on one of those posts. How did you do it?"

Clarissa's features changed to a thoughtful pose. *Click.* Dena took another picture.

"Daddy says it's in the wrist. He taught me." She beamed.

Click. "Well, your daddy must be pretty special. Smile for the camera."

Clarissa glowed. Dena clicked off two more shots. "All done."

"Really?"

"Really."

"Can I see the picture now?"

"No, sweetheart. This camera only takes pictures with film."

"Daddy's camera shows you the picture right away."

Dena chuckled and lifted the camera she was wearing around her neck for that occasional digital shot. "This camera works like your daddy's."

"Oh." Clarissa narrowed the distance between her eyebrows.

Clarissa's mother called out, "Come now, Clarissa, others are waiting."

Dena turned to Wayne Kearns and his. . .girlfriend? Wife? "What can I do for you this evening? The standard picture for the church or something more?"

"Jess and I would like to have a family portrait done."

Family portrait. He married the girl? Well, I suppose that's the proper thing to do. Forgive me, Lord. I'm doing it again. What is it about this man that unnerves me so? Possibly the fear of another pie attack, she reasoned. "Fine. Sit back here. I'll take the one for the church directory first. Did Misty show you the possible backgrounds?"

"Yes." He motioned for Jess to sit down, then stood behind her.

Dena looked through the lens of the camera as he placed his hands lovingly on the beautiful young woman's shoulders. "I'm sorry," Dena said. "Would you mind sitting, Wayne? You're too tall for Jess's height in the chair. The picture would be unbalanced."

"No problem," he answered.

Jess popped up from the chair. "See, I told you for years you were too tall. It has nothing to do with me being short."

Years? Just how young was she when he married her? Dena blinked away the thoughts and arranged the couple. "Place your hands on his shoulders like so," she instructed.

Jess obeyed.

"Relax a bit, Mr. Kearns."

"He hates having his picture taken," Jess supplied.

"Oh, do I need to tell you how pretty you are?"

Wayne's eyebrows shot up in shocked surprise.

Not funny! Dena chastised herself as she went behind her camera to refocus. *I can't believe I said that.* She wished she had an old Cirkut camera so she could drape its dark cloth over her head and hide.

Wayne crossed his arms.

Great. Real professional, Dena. "Okay, where are those smiles I saw earlier?" Dena coaxed.

Jess massaged Wayne's shoulders.

He reached up and patted Jess's hands, splashing a grin across his face that could charm any woman. "I'm doing this for you, honey."

Lord, help me, I'm attracted to a married man. She glanced down at his ring finger. Nothing. She glanced up at Jess's. A small silver band encircled it. *He didn't buy her gold? Who is this guy?*

"Thanks, Dad." Jess kissed the top of his head.

"Dad?" The word tumbled from Dena's lips before she could stop it. Heat warm enough to be a hot flash rose across her cheeks. But this had nothing to do with hormones.

Or did it?

three

Dena moved through the last of her customers as quickly as possible. As much as she would like a lobster dinner, she'd decided not to step foot in the church. She'd made a perfect fool of herself today. Tromping through the Florida Everglades fighting off alligators seemed more desirable than being here on the rocky coast of Maine.

Jason and Marie had been encouraging her to move up here. She'd even started to pack up her condo in Boston. But today proved she belonged in the city. *Lots of people, no one knows who you are, and you can live out your embarrassing moments in private.* She'd been offered more pieces of cream pie today than there were stars in the sky.

She put the last of her equipment in her backpack, collapsed the tripod, and headed for the car. Dena slammed the trunk closed and leaned against the back end, inhaling the cool night air. The stars played off a deep sea of midnight blue.

"Mrs. Russell."

Dena closed her eyes. She knew Wayne's voice. It rolled down her spine like the water rushing over her shoulders in the hot springs of North Carolina.

"I'm sorry about earlier today."

She didn't turn to greet him. "It was an accident, Mr. Kearns. Don't think a thing of it."

"Oh, I'll be hearing about how I creamed the pastor's mother for the rest of the year, I reckon."

Dena held back a giggle.

"I also apologize for the confusion in the photo booth."

She turned and faced him now. There he stood, six feet tall, with rugged shoulders and a face so handsome even the darkness couldn't cloak it. "I'm sorry. I don't know why I would assume she was anything but your daughter."

He took a step forward, his hands behind his back. His teeth flashed in a bright smile that set her insides quivering. *Stop these foolish thoughts,* she reprimanded herself, fighting for some semblance of control.

"It's flattering that you'd think someone as beautiful as Jess would be attracted to me."

"Actually, I was more concerned with something Jason had said about you working with the youth—"

Wayne let out a guffaw, then stopped the laughter. "I'm sorry. You're not from around here, so you wouldn't know she's my daughter. Jess is a senior at Gordon College."

"Congrats."

"I'm proud of her, as you probably could tell. Look, I figured you're feeling embarrassed enough, so I brought you something." He handed her a Styrofoam box. "I hope you like lobster."

"Thank you." She accepted the container. "I love it."

He glanced at the church, then back at her. "Great. Well, I hope you come and visit Squabbin Bay again sometime. Perhaps at a time when you can relax and not spend the day working."

"Actually, I'm staying for a few days." *Now why did I tell him that?*

"Wonderful. Enjoy your visit." He headed back to the church. "Oh, just for the record, you did a great job raising that boy of yours."

"Thank you." Jason had grown to be a fine man, and it was nice hearing it from the people the Lord had placed under his shepherding care. Perhaps she could move here after all.

She drove to the small cottage she'd been renting for the past couple of months. At the time it seemed like the logical thing to do. Admittedly, she'd only been able to visit twice. Her cell phone rang. "Hello?"

"Hey, Mom, I heard you were up at Jason's this weekend."

"Chad, where are you?" As a commercial pilot, her youngest son kept a schedule that always had him on the move.

"Fifty miles away. I'm coming up with someone I'd like you to meet."

Her grin broadened. Chad had been talking about Brianne for two years, but they'd only started dating a year ago. With him flying all over the country, it was hard for them to spend any real time together. "I have a spare room at the cottage, but you'll be bunking on the couch."

"Not too lumpy, I hope."

"Don't know. Never slept on it."

"Just came off a five-day trip. I could sleep on a rock. I was hoping to get up in time for Jason's church fair. How's it going? Is it over?"

"Fine. I had no idea *that* many people lived in Squabbin Bay. I left before it finished. I'm on my way to the cottage."

"Run out of film?"

Dena turned down the dirt road that led to her cottage. "Me? Never. Do you know how to get here?"

"More or less. I'll call you when I'm in town, and you can give me directions."

"Sure. I'll make up the bed for Brianne."

"Thanks, Mom. She's looking forward to meeting you."

She could hear the joy in her son's voice. Dena's confidence in the Lord that this was the right gal for Chad rose another notch. "I'm looking forward to meeting her, too. See you soon, son."

Dena pulled up to the remote, weathered, shingled cottage overlooking a small inlet. The moonlight danced on the water, and a whiff of salty air brushed past her nose. The powerful pull of the ocean renewed her as the surf crashed on the shore below.

Taking in a deep breath, she sighed and went into the quaint cottage. It had two small bedrooms, a bath, and a simple kitchen that opened into the living room. A modest table divided the two rooms. The cottage also sported a porch, which, at first, Dena had wished wasn't screened in, until she met her match in mosquitoes, black flies, and the numerous other flying insects. This seemed particularly ironic when she considered all the wilds she'd photographed. She set the camera backpack on the counter, made the bed in the guest room, and laid out some bedding for Chad near the couch. Thankfully, the house came fully furnished.

Moments later she set some water in the teakettle to boil and opened the dinner Wayne Kearns had packed for her. Lobster salad set on a bed of romaine lettuce. A fresh bun of Portuguese sweet bread and some green grapes rounded out her meal. "Perfect." She dove her fork in.

Her cell phone rang.

"Hello?"

"Hey, Mom, we just passed the church and are heading east on Main Street."

Dena gave directions between mouthfuls. When she finished eating, her stomach gurgled. She had polished off the church meal and began scavenging through the refrigerator looking for something more. A black and furry container sat in the back of the fridge, something from her last visit. With the tips of her fingers, she grabbed the furry creature and tossed it, container and all.

"Mom, I see a fork in the road."

"Back up; you missed the drive. There's no marker, and it's really tough to find." She tapped the refrigerator door shut. "Did you guys bring any food?"

"Just some junk food for the road. Why, are you hungry?" Chad asked.

"Starving!"

Chad laughed. "Worked hard, didn't you?"

Admittedly, she was famished after any full day of shooting. Her appetite always increased when she worked hard.

Thankfully, weight had never been an issue. Her own sister, Carrie, had a very different metabolism, forcing her to constantly watch her weight. "Kinda."

"Hey, I think I found it."

"Hang on, I'll turn the outside lights off and on." She stepped to the side door and flicked the switch up and down a couple of times.

"I see you. We'll be there in a minute."

"Great." Dena clicked her phone shut and went outside to greet them.

Chad's idea of junk food—almonds, dried fruit, and some bottled fruit juice—abated her hunger.

"Mom, Brianne and I have something to tell you."

❧

"Good morning, Dad. How many did you pull in this morning?" Jess sat at the breakfast table with a cup of tea and a bagel loaded with cream cheese.

"Ten. It's an off season, I guess."

"Bummer. I guess I can't hit you up for a fancy red sports car like Mrs. Russell's for a graduation present, huh?"

Wayne pulled out a chair at the table. "Never even considered it. In fact, I was starting to plan what kind of a gift you'd be getting me for your graduation."

"Huh?" The bagel in Jess's hand plopped back on the plate.

"You know, pay me back, thank me—those kinds of things. Personally, I'd like a '68 Mustang convertible in pristine condition."

"Dream on, Dad." Jess retrieved the fallen bagel and bit into it.

Wayne reached over and grabbed the other one off her plate.

"Hey, get your own." She swatted his hand.

"Why? You can make another for the both of us."

Jess rolled her eyes heavenward, picked up her plate, and headed for the kitchen. "Thanks for taking the picture with me."

"Not a problem, princess. So, tell me, besides senioritis, what's happening at school?" Wayne leaned against the counter and sampled the bagel. He couldn't help but be curious about one Mr. Trevor Endicott. *Having a historical New England name didn't necessarily mean he was a good man, and*—he continued to fret—*and, I don't like it that he's declined to meet with me three times throughout the past semester.*

Jess folded her arms across her middle. "What you're really asking about is Trev, isn't it?"

She had him there. "Yes. And everything else. You know me, Mr. Nosy Dad from way back." He tried not to be too nosy, and he tried to keep a balance between her need for privacy and his own responsibility to watch and protect her.

Jess's laughter eased the slight tension in the room. "You'll never change."

"Not likely." Wayne poured a cup of coffee. "Want one?" he asked, lifting the pot.

"No, thanks. I'm heading back to school right after church. I'll grab a cup there at the fellowship hall. Trev is taking me out to dinner tonight."

"Jess, I don't want to sound like a broken record—"

"Then don't. You need to trust me, Dad."

"It's not that I don't trust you. But it is odd that this young man has managed to avoid seeing me on three separate occasions. Doesn't that bother you?"

"Yes, but there've been very good reasons each and every time."

"I see. And what happened this time?" Wayne sipped his coffee and prayed for the Lord's leading. *Guide me, Lord.*

Jess plopped down at the kitchen table. "He was called into work to cover for someone."

"He couldn't say he had other plans?"

Jess nibbled her lower lip. Wayne took in a deep breath. *She's concerned, too.*

"Tell you what. I'll plan a trip down there next weekend

and take the two of you out to dinner."

"Really?" She jumped up from her seat.

"Sure. I understand what it is to work for a living."

"Thanks, Daddy. I'll tell Trev. He'll be so excited."

I hope so, Wayne prayed. The one thing that really got under his skin was anyone hurting his daughter.

"What did you think of Mrs. Russell, the pastor's mother?" Jess asked.

Where'd that come from? She sat there staring at him with a foolish grin on her face.

"She seemed like a nice person," he finally commented—not that he wanted his daughter to know he found the woman attractive.

"Hard to tell with all that cream on her face, huh?"

Wayne grabbed a hand towel and twisted it into a rat's tail. "You'd think I'd get a little respect from my own daughter." He snapped the towel.

Jess picked up another, and their mock battle ensued. He took aim and snapped the end of the towel at her knee. She countered with a snap at his elbow. They stopped after they were unable to stand up straight from their own laughter.

"Seriously, Dad. What did you think of Dena Russell? I saw you give her that plate of food."

❧

Dena stretched her stiff body as she got up from bed. She glanced at the alarm clock. The red digital glow of the numbers read ten o'clock. Dena moaned.

"Chad, Brianne, we overslept. Get up!" she called out before exiting the bedroom door. In the kitchen, she found the young couple snuggled up beside each other, sipping their coffee.

"You overslept, Mom." Chad's grin filled his face. His features were softer than Jason's, but she still saw Bill in both of her sons. "I was about to wake you. I tried an hour ago, but it was no use."

"Sorry." She'd been doing that more and more lately after

a hard day of work. Getting older definitely had a downside. She headed back to the bedroom. "I'll be ready in seven minutes, then we'll leave for church."

Chad and Brianne giggled. Dena tossed her head from side to side. *Young love.*

Showered and dressed, the small group went to church. Dena sat back in the old oak pew. Jason had told her that they'd been made from local lumber nearly three hundred years ago. Dena scanned the congregation. She'd photographed just about everyone.

"Grandma, Uncle Chad!" Billy yelped out, leaving the pew where he'd been with his mom.

"Shh," Dena warned.

Chad scooped the boy up in a bear hug. "Hey, buddy, how you doing?"

"Good. You should have been here yesterday. Dad got dunked over and over again."

The entire congregation started to chuckle.

"Oh, man, I wish I'd been here to see that. I wouldn't have minded dunking your daddy myself."

Billy leaned toward his uncle's ear. "Mr. John made it easy to dunk him," he said in a rather loud whisper.

Dena glanced over to John Dixon. *I wonder how Jason will get back at him.* She winked. John's wife buried her head deeper into her church bulletin.

Jason called the service to order. "Good morning, everyone. I trust all of you had a good time yesterday. We raised three thousand dollars for the youth ministries, thank the Lord."

A round of applause erupted.

Jason raised his hands to abate the praise. "Hang on, there's more good news to thank the Lord on." The room hushed. "Jessica Kearns informed me this morning that she will be graduating with honors from Gordon College in two weeks."

Dena scanned the congregation, looking for Wayne and his daughter, Jessica. The broad smile on her father's face showed just how proud he was.

"I'd say the college scholarship fund and investing in our youth has seen a long and good history in this church. With God's help, I pray we continue to be sensitive to the Lord's leading for our youth." Jason drew the congregation back to the purpose of their meeting, of fellowship with one another and fellowship with God.

Dena closed her eyes and silently prayed. It had been hard being a single mother, raising three kids through their teen years, supporting them, and still trying to be there when they came home from school. But her career choice had paid off. Purchasing the storefront with an upstairs apartment allowed her to have the studio at home and be near her children. And when they had grown and left for college, taking photo opportunities around the world for national magazines and other media groups had helped pay for their college educations. A tear edged her eye. *Thank You, Lord. Without Your help, I couldn't have done it. Now I'm blessed with two grown sons and a grown daughter, each of them making their own families.* Chad and Brianne's engagement and desire to marry quickly had startled her, but she was happy for them. After a long discussion, they'd decided to get married next weekend in Maine and honeymoon for a week in the Caribbean.

Church. She opened her eyes and focused on Jason. Out of the corner of her eye, she caught a glimpse of Wayne Kearns. Her heart fluttered. Her palms began to sweat. She closed her eyes and reopened them, staring straight ahead. She was a grown woman and had no time for romance.

She snuck another glance at the very handsome Wayne Kearns. *He's too young.* He looked over at her and smiled. Her cheeks flamed.

She closed her eyes and bowed her head. *Dear God in heaven, what's come over me?*

four

Wayne Kearns couldn't help but be amused by Dena Russell. She was a beautiful woman, even with whipped cream hanging off her nose. On the other hand, he felt guilty for having been the cause of her embarrassment. Jess had informed him that everyone brought or offered her a piece of pie throughout the entire fair. If Squabbin Bay was noted for anything apart from the lobster industry, it had to be that it was a town of practical jokers. And while he understood that, he wasn't too sure that the beautiful Mrs. Russell would. Pastor Russell had told him on more than one occasion how his mother had virtually raised him and his siblings alone.

Of course, Pastor Russell knew of Wayne's past, and being a single parent since the age of eighteen had been very difficult in the beginning.

He thought back on the service, to the brief moment when his gaze caught Dena's. Wayne shook off the memory and paced the deck overlooking his backyard. Once again the image of Dena's cream-covered face came into view.

Wayne stomped off the deck, over to his truck, and headed back to church. He'd planned to spend the afternoon with Jess, but she'd gone back to see her boyfriend. *Boyfriend!* Did he even like the sound of that word?

Wayne turned off the engine in the church parking lot. He pulled out his toolbox and marched into the fellowship hall. Within minutes he had the doors off their hinges and laid out on a couple of sawhorses. John Dixon was right; these doors needed windows.

"Hello!" Wayne heard someone call as he clicked off his jigsaw. He turned to greet the pastor. A slight heat rose on the

30

back of his neck.

"Hi. I decided to fix these doors."

Pastor Russell placed his hands on his hips. "Need a hand?"

"Not really. I can frame out the windows, but I don't have the glass to fill in the holes today."

Pastor Russell leaned over the door. "I see. Wouldn't it have been better to wait until you had the glass?" He chuckled.

"Probably. But my guilt got the best of me. I feel so badly about your mom. I heard that just about everyone brought her a piece of pie yesterday."

Jason Russell smiled. "Just about." He leaned back against the other sawhorse. "She can handle it."

Wayne sanded the edges of the pine frame he would place around the hole he'd cut for the window.

"Wayne, can I ask you something?"

"Sure, what's up?"

"Well, old Ben Costa said it's been a bad year for lobstering. Have you noticed?"

"Yeah, it happens every now and again. Why, is Ben hurting?"

"Some. The church has been able to help."

"I'll keep an eye out for him."

"Thanks. It isn't like he hadn't planned ahead for retirement."

Wayne left the sandpaper on the door and brushed off his hands. "Yeah, Maggie getting cancer really knocked out their savings. One thing about this community, people help one another."

"Very true. But if everyone's feeling the crunch with the low hauls this year. . ." Pastor Jason looked up at the ceiling and let his words hang for a moment. "We could be in for an interesting year."

Wayne nodded. He lobstered, but he also worked as a carpenter. With a daughter to raise, he couldn't afford the lean seasons of fishing only.

"Jason," Dena Russell called while entering the room.

"I'm coming, Mom." Pastor Russell turned back. "Sorry,

I told the family I'd only be a minute. My brother, Chad, is getting married next weekend."

"Congratulations."

"Thanks, now to figure out how to do premarital counseling in a week." Pastor Russell slapped Wayne on the back. "Thanks for the windows."

"You're welcome."

Dena stood in the doorway.

"Hi," he said.

"Hi."

Wayne looked down at the door lying in front of him.

"Peace offering?" she asked.

"Kinda. I had the afternoon free, and, well, while I might have innocently creamed you with a pie, what would have happened if it were a small child?"

"Ah, I see your point." She glanced back at Pastor Russell exiting the building. "Could you use a hand?"

Her smile sent a kicker of a punch deep in his gut. "Sure," he managed to speak. Wayne found himself in unfamiliar territory. For years, he'd been too busy to consider a relationship. Now, in less than twenty-four hours, he found himself unable to think of anything but getting to know this woman.

"What can I do?"

"Could you sand the rough edges off this framing?"

"Sure." She took the sandpaper and began to work.

Wayne paused for a moment and caught himself staring. He walked over to the other door and cut open the hole for the window.

A few minutes later, Dena asked, "Are we staining or painting?"

"I'll stain to go with the original."

"Okay, where's the stain?"

"Didn't bring any. I'll take care of that later in the week after I can get to the store and purchase the stain and glass."

She nodded and sat down on a chair.

"Pastor Russell said he was trying to convince you to move up here."

Dena chuckled. "Yes, he is."

"What's keeping you in the city?"

"Convenience, mostly. I travel a lot for my work, and Logan, in spite of the traffic, is a good airport for foreign travel."

"From what your son says, you're on the road a lot."

"Yeah, he's trying to get me to slow down a bit. Personally, I wouldn't mind, but each new trip is exciting, a new world to explore and photograph. I love it."

Wayne lined up the angled cut for the corners of the frame for the second door. "I haven't been any farther than Boston. I've lived down east in Squabbin Bay all my life. I've seen many photographs of places I would love to see someday. But more than likely, I won't get much farther than various spots in New England."

The small board slipped.

Dena stood before him. "Can I hold the board for you?"

"Thanks." He could smell the light lavender scent of her perfume. *Perhaps she should stay in Boston.*

☙

"Why did I offer to help him, Lord?" Dena spoke out loud in the security of her automobile. With Chad and Brianne now getting married in Squabbin Bay, she'd have to stay for the week. "A wedding in a week. Lord, is the end of the world at hand and I don't know about it?"

On the other hand, the kids made sense. Their schedules conflicted so often, it was impossible for the two of them to have much time off together.

Dena went over the list of things she needed to do. She placed the phone's hands-free headset to her ear and started her calls while driving to the market to purchase some food. She'd have to travel to Boston for appropriate wedding clothing. She drummed her fingernails on the steering wheel. *What to wear?*

"Hello?"

"Hi, Jamie. It's Dena Russell."

"Hey, Dena, what's happening?"

"A ton. I'm wondering if you'd like to cover an assignment for me." Dena filled in the eager photographer about the assignment in Australia.

"Thanks so much. I owe you."

"Just do me proud and come back with some excellent shots."

"I promise. Thanks. Thanks again."

"You're welcome."

"Bye." Jamie hung up the phone.

The rest of the day, Dena found herself busy making wedding plans, rearranging her schedule, and trying to figure out when to develop the pictures she'd taken the day before at the church fund-raiser.

By nightfall she found herself with a cup of black coffee, sitting on the deck, looking out over the bay. Crickets chirped and the stars shone their brilliance.

Wayne's handsome green eyes floated back in her memory. They seemed to appear overhead in the night sky. "Lord, what's wrong with me? Why am I attracted to a man I don't even know?"

The phone rang.

Dena jumped up and answered it. "Hello?"

"Hi, Mom." Amber's voice sounded cheery but tired.

"Hi, honey. What's up?"

"You mean besides Chad's rush wedding? He's so Chad. It's a good thing he flies jets; nothing else would be fast enough for him."

Dena laughed. "Agreed. So, to what do I owe the pleasure of hearing your sweet voice tonight?"

"David and I have a slight problem."

"Money?"

"Yeah, sorry, but can you help us out again?"

"Sure, I'll pay for the trip. You don't have to pay me back. Also, I'll rent another cottage for the weekend for your whole family."

"No, Mom, we can make do at your place."

"Maybe you can, but I can't. I love you, but this place is too small for five extra people. Not to mention Chad will be staying here, too."

"Ah, well, I hate for you to pay so much."

"Amber, it'll be my pleasure. My present to Chad. After all, he doesn't need a lot of wedding gifts. He's had his own place for years and has made good money."

"True." Amber's voice lowered. "David's overcoming the layoff, but he's so worried and depressed about our finances."

Dena spent a few minutes trying to encourage Amber about her and David's financial situation. There were many days, shortly after Bill died, when she didn't think she would be able to survive and keep the family intact. But the Lord had provided, and, after many years, He provided above and beyond what she ever expected.

"Jason says you had a run-in with a cream pie."

"Yeah, and this town is a bunch of pranksters. Just about every one of them came up to me with a slice of pie afterward. The poor man who hit me felt so guilty he was at the church this afternoon putting windows in the doors where it happened."

Amber's laughter reminded Dena of when Amber was a teen still living at home.

"I heard he nearly ruined Old Faithful."

"Don't remind me. The only thing that probably helped me keep my cool was that my camera didn't get damaged. Wayne's handsome green eyes wouldn't have been sparkling then."

"Handsome. . ." Amber paused. "Green eyes."

Horror rushed over Dena. Why had she ever expressed her inner thoughts to her daughter?

"Tell me more, Mom."

"Nothing to tell," she fumbled through her words.

"Uh-huh. You're attracted to the pie man."

"Amber, please. I merely said he had handsome eyes, and you know how I've always loved green eyes. I've photographed hundreds, but I've never fallen in love with any."

"Love." Amber sobered. "Mom, are you all right?"

"I'm fine, sweetheart. No problem about the money; it's a gift for Chad. Let David know that is how I'm looking at it."

"Thanks again, Mom." Amber giggled. "And I'll be praying about your handsome, green-eyed pie man. Maybe there will be another wedding in the family."

"Huh. Nope, all of you will be hitched after Chad ties the knot with Brianne. That's it; no one else to marry off."

"Mom." Amber paused. "Isn't it possible the Lord might want you to have another helpmate? I mean, Daddy's been gone for nearly twenty years. Wouldn't it be nice to have someone to talk to and be with now that we're all grown and married?"

Dena leaned her head against the wall in the kitchen. "I don't know, Amber. I've been single most of my life. And I'm rather set in my ways. I'm not sure I want someone interrupting my routine."

"Fair enough. Love ya, Mom, and thanks."

"You're welcome." Dena listened to the dial tone on the phone for a moment before she hung up the receiver. *Love. Marriage. Companionship. Do I want those, Lord?*

Wayne's handsome image replayed in her mind for the umpteenth time tonight.

Dena took in a deep breath. *Stop being a foolish old woman,* she admonished. The roll of the surf echoed through the night air. *A stroll on the beach will help me clear my mind. I hope.*

&

Wednesday morning met Wayne with continued frustrations. The lobstering was more than bad this year—it was downright ridiculous. He pulled in only five keepers. He scanned the gray ocean as fog drifted over the sea. A call to the local game and fisheries warden was in order. It didn't seem possible they'd overfished the lobsters in Squabbin Bay, but. . . Wayne removed his cap and rubbed the back of his neck.

He scanned the coast and saw a figure walking along the beach. *I wonder if it's Dena Russell.* He turned the wheel and headed his boat toward shore. Ever since he met one Dena Russell, his mind had been tossing around the idea of dating like a loose buoy floating on the waves.

He put the engine to idle and leaned over to pick up another one of his buoys. Again, he found the pot empty. He filled the bait bag and tossed the pot overboard.

Another skiff peeked out of the fog. *Who's that?* he wondered. He watched for a moment to see if he recognized the vessel. But the fog was too thick, and the boat slipped farther into the gray mist. *That's odd.* He set the boat in gear and debated about going closer to shore. The cottage she had rented was on top of the cliff. And who else would have such a huge camera lens, except for a professional?

He eased the boat closer toward shore and squeezed the air horn.

Dena turned and focused on him. He brought the boat a bit closer. She walked toward him.

"Hi," he called out.

"Hi. You're lobstering?" she asked.

"Trying—not too many today."

"Which buoys are yours?"

He pointed out. "The red with a silver stripe." Each fisherman had his own color design on his buoys so they were easily identified one from another.

"Perhaps you should not pull the same pots as your partner." She grinned. "You might catch more."

"Partner?" Wayne aimed the boat toward shore and cut the engine. "What partner?"

five

Dena watched Wayne toss an anchor and secure the line. "What do you mean, a partner?" he asked. "I don't have a partner; haven't for years."

But hadn't she seen someone. . . ? "I thought I saw someone pulling a pot earlier with those markings."

"How? Is that a telephoto lens?" He stood on the boat as if he were a part of it. His body shifted with the waves as the boat bounced up and down in the mild surf.

"Yes. And yes, I did notice him through the lens."

"Did you snap a picture?"

"No, I'm afraid not, why?"

Wayne rubbed the back of his neck. "Because if you did see someone pulling up my pots, they were stealing."

"Oh, sorry, no." Now why hadn't she taken a snapshot of the man? *Because it was gray and not a very picturesque photograph,* she reminded herself.

"Guess that would have been too easy." Wayne hiked up his hip boots and slipped over the stern of the boat.

"I'm sorry. I didn't have any reason to believe the person was doing anything illegal." Dena felt foolish. She'd witnessed a crime but knew little. She hadn't even paid that much attention to the details of the boat or the man's clothing, nothing. She'd been too busy thinking about another lobsterman, the one before her right now.

"I and a few other lobstermen have been having a bad year. If we have a poacher, that could explain it. Besides me, only Ben Costa has pots in this area."

"I'll be happy to watch, and if I see anything, I'll photograph it."

He let out a deep breath. "Thanks. I doubt whoever it is will be back this week. But you never know. How early were you out here?"

Dena looked down at the small patch of sand on this relatively rocky coastline. "I was up at four. I thought I'd get some sunrise shots in."

"Sun doesn't rise 'til close to six. What woke you up so early?"

Of course, a fisherman would know when the sun rises. Dena cleared her throat. "Unable to sleep."

"Dena, I—" He coughed. "I was wondering if you'd like to go to dinner one night this week."

Dena wrapped her waist with her arms and braved looking straight into Wayne's handsome green eyes. "I—" What did she want to say? That she was a widow and didn't date? What kind of an excuse was that? "I don't date," she stammered.

"Oh, well, I haven't been on one since the last time my sister set me up on a blind date fourteen years ago. So, I guess I'm really asking for you to join me for dinner. More of an opportunity to get to know one another at a time when a pie isn't involved."

Dena chuckled. "No pie is a good plan." She wanted to get to know this man. More than that, her prayer time had been filled with prayers for him and Jess. For her upcoming graduation and the changes that would happen to their small family after she graduated.

Dena remembered all too well what it was like when Jason graduated college and Amber left home to live on campus. But the final blow had been when Chad enlisted in the armed services. Through the air force, he had gained his college education and his flying experience.

She locked her gaze back on Wayne. "All right, I'd love to."

A smile creased his ruggedly handsome face. "Great. How's tonight?"

"Jason has a midweek prayer meeting."

"Right. I forgot it was Wednesday. I could pick you up

before the meeting, and we could go together."

Heat washed over her body. "This is a small town, right?"

He knitted his eyebrows, then they rose slightly. "Oh, yeah. I forgot. Okay, we could go to the restaurant in separate cars. . . . Wait, that won't matter. Half the town will see us at the restaurant anyway."

Dena chuckled. "True. All right, let's light up those phone lines tonight and arrive at the church together. If I'm going to make a fool of myself. . ." She couldn't believe she let that much of her inner thoughts slip out.

Wayne reached over and grasped her hand. "Dena, I've got to be honest. I'm attracted to you, but I'm scared. I'm an old man set in my ways."

"Old? You? Do you have any idea how old I am? Far too old for dating or even. . ." She cut herself off.

"You can't be a day over thirty-nine." He winked.

"Hmm, that would put me at the ripe old age of six when I had Jason."

Wayne let out a low chuckle, then his gaze met hers. "We're both old enough not to mince words. Let's see if this is something the Lord is doing in our lives."

"Agreed." Yes, the Lord needed to be central in this relationship, if there was even going to be a relationship. Perhaps she was just jumping the gun. Perhaps the Lord had intended for them simply friendship, nothing more. "When should I be ready?"

"Five forty-five."

"That's precise."

"It's the Yank in me." He grinned.

They said their good-byes, and Dena watched him pilot his boat out of the inlet. The fog had lifted, and a bright blue sky emerged. "Okay, Lord." She looked toward heaven and held out her hands. "It's Your move."

Fear knotted in her stomach. She let out a long sigh. "Give me peace, Lord."

⊱

After returning his boat to the harbor, Wayne spent the rest of the morning finishing the Gallager job. His mind focused more on the upcoming evening than on the job at hand. He nailed and renailed the railing five times. If he kept that up, he'd be paying the customer.

He stopped by old Ben Costa's house and talked with him about this year's fishing. Wayne noted that his hauls were similar to Ben's, small and decreasing weekly. Then he stopped by his parents' house and turned over their garden in time for their summer visit. By four o'clock he needed a shower and some serious time to get ready for his date.

Date. The word nearly lodged in his throat. After all these years, he finally asked someone on a—he coughed. "Date." He took the stairs two at a time and sealed himself off in his bathroom.

He pulled out a pair of jeans and an off-white cable-knit sweater, one his mother had knitted for him years ago. A pair of leather Top-Siders, and he had his outfit. He glanced in the mirror. "Show the real you, Wayne. Or it's not even worth her time or yours," he challenged himself.

At five o'clock he made his normal midweek call to Jess. "Hi, honey. How you doing?" he asked.

"Fine, Dad. I'm cramming for my archaeology exam."

"I'll say a prayer for you tonight."

"Thanks. Trev said he's looking forward to seeing you on Saturday."

"Great, I'm looking forward to meeting this man."

They talked for another ten minutes about her week, finals, and how full her schedule was. Graduation ceremonies were days away. Wayne planned on attending everything a parent could.

"Well, I've got to go, sweetheart."

"Okay. Short call tonight, what's up? Everyone's okay, aren't they?" she inquired.

"Everyone's fine. I—" Did he dare tell her that he had a dinner date? "I made plans to join someone for dinner."

"Great—give Bob and Wendy my love."

Was he that predictable that his daughter knew everything about him? Or at least she thought she did. "Actually, I'll be going out with Mrs. Russell—"

He pulled the phone from his ear as Jess shrilled out, "All right, Dad!"

After they said good-bye, he hung up the phone and grabbed his keys from the kitchen table. His old truck with faded blue paint didn't look like a vehicle one would use to escort a woman on a date. On the other hand, he was going to be himself. And part of who he was rolled on four wheels and served a function. It wasn't his top priority. That was his daughter, his blessing from God, a true miracle. The message of grace played out day after day in his life, seeing the way the Lord took his mistakes and washed them and turned them into blessings. "You're awesome, Lord. Keep me from worrying about my appearance tonight. Help me focus on just being myself."

❧

"Hello?" Dena answered the phone.

"Hi, Mom. Marie said she forgot to invite you for dinner tonight. If you haven't made anything yet, you're welcome to come on over."

"Thanks, Jason, but I'm busy." Dena curled the phone cord around her first finger. *How does a woman tell her grown son she's going out on a date?*

"Okay, I'll see you later."

"Later." Dena hung up the phone and glanced at the clock. She had five minutes, if her clock was set the same as his. Tires crunched the oyster-shelled driveway. *Guess not*, she mused.

Years of travel made her aware of how flexible time could be for some cultures. But Wayne said he was a Yank, and New

Englanders typically arrived five to ten minutes before they were expected, in order to be on time. She walked over to the kitchen door that met the driveway and opened it.

He stepped out of his truck wearing blue jeans and an off-white fisherman's sweater. She laughed. She was wearing the same outfit.

"What's so funny?" Wayne examined himself, twisting around, looking for something that might be hanging off his backside.

"Nothing. We just have similar tastes in clothing."

His gaze landed back on her. His lips thinned and turned up at the corners of his mouth. "Who made your sweater? My mom knitted this one years ago."

"I purchased it in Scotland."

"You have seen the world, haven't you?"

"Not completely, but, yes, I've traveled quite a bit." He stood there a step below her. The top of his head was covered with a myriad of curls. She stepped back into the kitchen. "Come in. I'm just about ready."

Wayne entered the house with a confident stride. *Why am I so nervous? Wayne doesn't seem to be,* she pondered. "Make yourself comfortable. I'll be back in a sec."

"No problem. I forgot to ask, where would you like to go?"

"You name it." She headed to the bedroom. "It's your town; wherever you recommend will be fine with me." *Get ahold of yourself, girl. You're fifty-two years old and butterflies flew out a long time ago.* At least she thought they had. *Okay, face it. You're attracted to him. Now get a grip,* she scolded herself.

Facing the mirror, she slipped on the only pair of earrings she'd brought up for this trip—pearls. They blended well with the sweater, but normally she would have put in something darker that would offset her jeans. *Oh well, it's not a beauty pageant. Just a casual dinner.* "Ha," she quipped out loud. A final brush of her hair, and she had primped as much as she could. After all, he was in the other room and waiting.

"Okay, Lord, guide us." She opened the door and saw him staring out the sliding glass door, looking out over the ocean. "It's a beautiful view, isn't it?"

"Yes." He turned and faced her. "Both of them."

They stood for a moment in an awkward pause. He cleared his throat. "We better get going so we're not late for church."

"Good idea." She scooped up her Bible and followed him to the door. He held it open for her.

A gentleman. "Thanks. Would you like to take my car or yours?"

His smile faded. She watched his eyes go back and forth from her car to his truck. It took a moment, but then it hit her. Her red Mercedes convertible to his old truck shouted volumes. "I don't mind going in your truck."

His shoulders straightened. "I'm fine with either; you pick."

She stepped toward his truck. "Then yours; we won't have to shuffle vehicles." She hoped she didn't sound like a snob. The Mercedes had been the one vice she'd allowed herself. She'd been making good money for the past few years, and it had always been her dream car. She loved driving it up to Maine from Boston. So often it stayed parked in the garage.

"It's not much, but it runs well," he weakly offered.

"Wayne, don't misread my offer about the car. I'm as comfortable in a truck as I am in my car."

He nodded.

She didn't have a lot of money, but she made a comfortable living. The price of the Mercedes had been a real bargain, and she figured that if she treated it right, she'd have the car for twenty years, maybe more. It felt like a frugal investment at the time, but right at this moment, she wondered.

"I suppose I'm a little sensitive about my truck." He chuckled. He opened the passenger door for her. "It just seemed wiser to keep this one, do the work myself, and have a few more dollars to help Jess pay for her college education."

"Makes sense to me." She stepped up and sat down on the

bench seat. He scooted around the truck and entered the driver's side. "I didn't even have a car seven years ago. I was still helping the kids with their schooling."

"How many children do you have?" he asked as he turned on the engine.

"Three. Jason is my oldest; he's thirty-three. Amber lives in Nashua with her husband and three children. Chad, who you might have met on Sunday, is my baby."

"Jess is my only. I'm not sure I could have handled more than one," he stated.

"They can be a handful. Bill died when Jason was only thirteen. Raising three kids through their teen years on my own was tough at times."

"I can imagine."

The tension between them dissipated quickly. Dena relaxed, and she sensed Wayne was relaxing, too. "I bought the Mercedes five years ago. It was my dream car. I hardly get to drive it, which is why I don't mind driving up to Squabbin Bay every once in a while to see the kids."

"My dream car is a classic Mustang convertible."

Dena laughed. "That was my second choice. But unlike you, I don't work on cars, and I figured that I'd have a pretty hefty maintenance bill on a car like that."

"True, if you can't do the work yourself."

He pulled into a small parking lot. The restaurant sat on a bluff overlooking the ocean. "Squabbin's has the best seafood in town. But it also has a healthy turf menu."

"Sounds great. I'm starving."

He cupped her elbow and led her into the restaurant. *Yes,* she thought, *we definitely could become close friends.*

six

Dena sat stiffly beside him in his truck.

"That wasn't too bad, was it?" he asked.

Dinner had been wonderful. They found they were similar in their life views and personal tastes. Arriving together at church raised more than a few eyebrows. Wayne thought Pastor Russell almost fell over. One stern look from Dena, and Pastor Russell cleared his throat and continued the prayer meeting. She must have been quite a disciplinarian, he mused.

She let out a deep sigh. "Not too. I probably should have told Jason my dinner plans. It might have lessened the shock."

"I thought I saw the teenager in him ready to protect his mother."

Dena chuckled. "You did. Jason took on a lot of responsibility. I purchased a studio with an apartment in the upstairs with the insurance money I received after Bill died. So, while I was close at hand, Jason had the responsibility of watching the kids while I worked."

"Ah, so he became the man of the house."

"Yeah. I tried to avoid it as much as possible by encouraging him to go out for some sports. But it still happens, as much as you try to prevent it. Older children are just naturally protective of the one parent who's survived."

"Jess tried to mother me for a while. I think all kids go through a phase. But in my case, her mother married when Jess was eight, and by the time she was ten, she'd only receive an occasional card from her. It's sad, really, but Terry wasn't ready to be a mother."

"The divorce must have been hard. I'm sorry."

"Terry and I never married. All part of my unsaved past, I'm afraid. We were in high school. I was a senior and she was a sophomore. And, well, one thing led to another and she was pregnant. I told her I'd raise the baby if she didn't abort it, and she agreed. At first Terry tried to be a part of Jess's life, but she still had to finish high school. Her parents strongly encouraged her to go to college, and, well. . .she started slipping away from Jess then.

"Jess and I have talked about it many times. She's a good kid. She understands it wasn't anything she'd done, but that her mother was just a kid herself."

"I'm sorry, I didn't know."

Wayne let out a nervous chuckle. "No reason you should have. I'll tell you one thing, becoming a single father at eighteen made it real clear that premarital sex was not only wrong, it had consequences. I don't think I could have raised her without my parents' support. I was twenty by the time I let the Lord into my life."

He eased the truck down the dirt road that led to Dena's cottage. "What about you? When did you get saved?"

"I was thirteen, but I didn't get really serious until college. I've found my faith deepens with each new season in my life. When Bill died and I was alone to raise three kids, I struggled. Why did God take him? Why didn't we buy more life insurance? All those kinds of questions, and more. But looking back, I see that God was always with me, always leading me in the right direction. Of course, I didn't always listen and had to learn a few lessons the hard way." The lilt of her laughter warmed him.

He set the transmission in park.

"Would you like to come in for a glass of iced tea?" she offered.

He was exhausted, but he didn't want the evening to end. He enjoyed her company. "I'd love to."

Dena's cell phone rang. Wayne stayed seated in the truck.

"Hello?" she answered then stiffened. "I just got home; I'll call you later." She listened. "Right. Okay, talk to you tomorrow."

Wayne shifted his torso and turned toward her. "Pastor Russell?"

Dena nodded.

"I don't have to come in for the iced tea," he offered.

"No, don't be silly. He's just curious and he can wait."

Wayne smiled. "I left my cell phone at home. Jess knows I had dinner plans with you, so I'm certain I have a message waiting for me."

"Do you think they'll want to chaperone?"

"Probably, but they wouldn't dare say it. They'd want to, but—"

Laughter filled the cab. Dena laughed so hard, tears edged her eyes.

"Come on, let's get that iced tea and sit on the porch." Dena pulled the door handle before he had a chance to open it for her.

"Sounds wonderful." Wayne slipped out of the cab and stretched. "There's a little chill in the air tonight."

They reached the kitchen door and found a note attached. "What's this?" Dena pulled it down and scanned the contents.

"Anything the matter?" he asked.

"No, not really. The owner has decided to sell the place, so he's giving me fair warning."

"Ah, I knew Troy was thinking of moving down to South Carolina. Guess he decided. Can't blame him—his daughter's there, and the weather up here is hard on older folks."

Dena placed the note on the kitchen counter and retrieved two tall glasses. "You know, hot cocoa might be nicer with the temperature dropping."

"I'd love some."

"Great." She moved through the kitchen with an elegant grace. She fascinated him on so many levels. Each time he discovered something new about her, it just made him want to know more.

"Dena?"

"Huh?" She filled the teakettle with some water and placed it on the stove.

"I've had a wonderful evening tonight."

"Me, too." He watched as she bent slightly and turned on the gas flame, adjusting it to the size of the kettle.

"I think. . ." He paused.

What did he think? That he loved her? No, it's too soon—he couldn't fall in love after one date.

"I'd like to go out with you again." There. He said it.

She leaned back against the counter and crossed her legs at her ankles. "Truthfully, I'd like that, too."

His countenance brightened.

"But." She held up a finger. "I'm far too busy the rest of the week, and after the wedding I desperately need to go to Boston and take care of business. I was supposed to be in Australia this week."

"Oh, so when will you be back again?"

"I don't know; maybe three weeks."

He took a step closer and reached for her hand. "Can we plan on getting together when you return?"

A gentle smile curled her lips. "I'd like that."

The kettle whistled, stopping him from raising her hand to his lips.

≈

That Thursday morning Dena had awakened feeling more centered than she had in years. She liked Wayne and had really enjoyed their time together. They'd surprised themselves by talking till after midnight. A part of her wished she could have spent more time with him the rest of the week, but Chad's wedding had taken up every bit of her free time. Chad had picked up the various pieces of camera equipment she needed to photograph the wedding from her Boston apartment, as well as a suitable dress for the mother of the groom.

After the wedding she'd returned to Boston. By the end of the following week, Dena found herself longing for another date with Wayne. She called her landlord in Maine and asked him what he wanted for the property. Finding it a more-than-fair asking price, she agreed to purchase it. Jason was right; she needed to slow down.

Dena tapped out Wayne's home phone number.

"Hello." Hearing his voice helped soothe her nerves.

"Hi, it's Dena."

"Dena, I'm so glad you called. How are you?"

"Fine, busy. I'm sorry, but I won't be able to get up there for a month."

"Oh."

She could hear his disappointment. "I was wondering if you could do me a favor."

"Sure, what do you need?"

"Well, as you know, Jason wants me to move up there." She curled the phone cord around her finger. "I'm afraid I can't do that just yet, and I'm not sure I'll ever completely be able to move up there, but I did take a positive step. At least, I think it's a positive step."

"You're rambling," he chortled. The lilt of his laughter sent a shiver from behind her ear to the back of her neck.

"Right. Well, I purchased the cottage from Troy."

"I heard."

"Oh, right, small town. Anyway, what I'm thinking is, if I'm going to stay there for any length of time, I'll need a darkroom added to the cottage."

"Sounds reasonable."

"That's where you come in. Can you draw up some plans and give me an estimate?"

"Sure."

"I'm not looking for anything fancy but something functional, and possibly something that would not detract from the charm of the cottage. Is that possible?"

"I can work on it. But I've never put in a darkroom. Don't you need sinks and stuff like that?"

"Yes. I can send you some plans from my darkroom here. That should give you a good idea of the space and things I need."

"Sounds good. Dena, let's be careful we don't develop just a business relationship."

"I know it sounds like I might be trying to create distance between us, but I looked over my summer commitments, and I really can't get out of them without putting several companies in a jam."

"I understand. But—"

"Let's not just talk business," she finished for him.

"Right."

She could picture his handsome smile in her mind. "Oh, I have a gift for you and Jess."

"What?"

"It's a surprise. You'll just have to wait."

Wayne laughed. "Just don't make me wait too long."

"Not too long, I promise. As soon as I can get up there, I'll be there. It's a six-hour drive, so just driving up for one night seems a bit foolish, don't you think?"

"Depends on what you're driving up for."

"Touché." Dena uncurled the cord from her forefinger. "Wayne, is it silly to say I've missed you?"

"No more than for me to admit the same."

Dena thought for the hundredth time, how could their schedules blend? He lived in Maine, she in Boston. Traveling abroad would put a definite strain on any relationship they could develop. "Wayne, how's this going to work?"

"I don't know, Dena. One step at a time, I guess. What if we call one another once or twice a week and just talk?" he suggested.

"I'd like that."

"Dena, I hate to bring this call to a close, but I've got to run. The sheriff just pulled up."

"Sheriff?"

"Yeah, we're trying to figure out who's poaching our lobsters."

"Okay. As soon as I figure out when I can get back, I'll let you know."

"Great. Thanks for calling. Bye."

"Bye." Dena let the phone fall from her fingertips back into its cradle. *I wish I had taken photos of that lobsterman when I saw him. But I didn't know anything was wrong.*

❧

Wayne's brief meeting with the sheriff produced little. If only Dena had photographed the poachers. But "if only" washed out with the tide and meant nothing—merely empty thoughts that produced little except more frustration.

The desire to call Dena and continue their conversation caused him to hesitate by the phone for a moment. Then he remembered her request for an addition on the cottage.

It still boggled his mind that she could just purchase a place at the drop of a hat. Then again, land in the area didn't bring a premium asking price. In some ways, he wanted to ask Pastor Russell about his mother, to learn who she was and how often she traveled. Obviously a photographer made more money than he thought.

Money. He'd have to guard his heart about that. He had struggled for years when Jess was first born. And even today, while he lived comfortably enough, he still supported himself with two jobs. Of course, there was the cost of private college tuition.

Lord, the danger I see is that I could be jealous of Dena's money and her ability to just go anywhere at a moment's notice. Or purchase a house just for an occasional getaway. He continued to pray and worked his way out to his truck.

He picked up a spare key from Troy and went to the cottage to get a closer look. It was a typical summer cottage with little insulation. *If Dena is going to stay here in the winter, she might want something warmer.* He tapped the figures on the yellow legal-size pad of paper with his pencil.

For a few thousand more than the cost of the darkroom addition, he could raise the roof and add a loft for a master bedroom suite with a wonderful view of the ocean. Probably more than a few thousand—more like another ten. It was something he would do if he owned the place. But who knew how long she'd want to keep the property?

Wayne called Pastor Russell. With greetings aside, he asked, "Could you give me your mother's home phone number? I'm at her cottage, and she asked me to do some remodeling."

"Sure, just a minute." Wayne heard some papers rustling. "Area code 617. . ." As he continued, Wayne scribbled it down on the legal pad.

"Thanks."

"Not a problem. Tell Mom I'll be calling later about Amber."

"Sure." Wayne wondered what was going on with Dena's daughter but figured it wasn't his place to ask.

A few moments later, he tapped out Dena's number and put it in the phone's directory. When her machine answered, Wayne left a message and his cell phone number.

"Lord, I wish she didn't have to work so much." He glanced back up to the rafters. And here he was thinking of suggesting she increase her renovation budget. *Better stick to basics, or I'll never see the woman.*

After a few final measurements, he went back home to an empty house. Jess would be home for a few weeks after graduation, then she was off to begin her career. Working out of Boston. Perhaps he should consider visiting Boston more often.

His cell phone rang. Dena's name appeared on the display. His heart skipped a beat. "Hi," he answered.

"Hi, sorry I missed your call. What's up?"

"I went to your place and have some basic ideas I'd like to bounce off of you regarding the location of the darkroom."

"Sure, go ahead."

Wayne outlined three different options.

"Hmm, I kinda like the idea of an additional bedroom. The place is so small. Of course, I didn't buy it for the cottage as much as for the view."

"Yeah, it's a phenomenal view. In fact, I was dreaming and thinking it would be nice to add a second floor and build a master bedroom suite over the darkroom."

"That sounds wonderful. How much would it cost?"

"Off the top of my head, I'd say another ten."

"Hmm. That's sounds really nice. Let's go with it."

Why didn't I keep my mouth shut? She'll be on another trip to pay for this. "It's your dollar."

"Right." She sighed. "I suppose if I took that month-long photo shoot in Africa, I could afford it."

That was exactly what I wanted to avoid. "Dena, I. . ." He paused.

"Yeah, I know."

"What?"

"That it would be longer between times when we could see one another."

"Exactly. It's strange how easily we can finish each other's sentences, and we barely know one another."

"Strange is an understatement. It's downright scary. Why after all these years, am I even interested in spending time with a man?"

Wayne chuckled. "My charming personality, of course."

"And humbleness," she quipped.

"Seriously, I should mention that Jess is taking a job in Boston. So I'll probably be traveling down there every now and again."

"Where is she going to live?"

"I don't know. She's hoping she and a group of her friends can find a place together. Personally, I think they should have started looking a few months before graduation, but you know kids."

"Right—they have all the answers."

"And for some odd reason, things work out for them at a moment's notice. I never understood that. Of course, when I was their age, I never did anything foolish."

"Of course not." They laughed in unison. "Seriously, Wayne, if she needs a place to stay for a bit, she's welcome to spend some time in the spare room at my condo."

"That's awfully generous of you. I'll let her know."

"Generous? Don't be too sure. I might be hoping for her to be paid a visit by her handsome father."

"You think I'm handsome?"

Wayne chuckled under his breath as he heard Dena groan. *She hadn't planned on letting that slip out, either*, he mused.

seven

Four days later, Dena still couldn't believe the words she'd allowed to slip out. Since that call, she'd been arguing with herself—and the Lord—about the wisdom of building a relationship with Wayne.

"But he's a stranger, Lord," she argued once again. Dena tapped the computer keys and pulled up her schedule for the next week. "Where can I steal the time?"

She'd planned a trip to Savannah, Georgia, for a magazine layout that was due by the end of next week. Then the idea hit her. She dialed Wayne's cell phone number.

Dena glanced back at her schedule. "Wayne, are you busy tomorrow morning?"

"Not too; what are you thinking?"

"I'll drive up tonight and we can have breakfast together. I'll have to leave tomorrow afternoon in order to catch an early flight out of Boston."

"That seems like a lot of driving for a breakfast date."

"Ah, but you haven't tasted my lobster omelet."

Wayne chuckled. "Tell you what, I'll bring the lobster."

"I was counting on that." Dena smiled.

"When do you think you'll get here tonight?" he asked.

"Close to ten, I think; sooner if possible."

"Drive safely. I'll put the lobsters and some fresh food in the refrigerator for you."

"Thanks, not too much or it will spoil."

"Gotcha." He paused. "Call me if you get sleepy on the road."

"Thanks. Bye."

"Until tomorrow, bye."

Dena's phone rang as soon as she hung up. "Hello?"

56

"Dena, hi, it's Jamie."

"Hi, Jamie. How was Australia?"

"Awesome. I can't thank you enough for the opportunity. But I feel I owe you a portion of the contract. That was a pretty healthy paycheck."

Dena knew exactly how much she'd given up, but she had to be there for Chad's wedding. "No problem. Your bailing me out on short notice is payment enough."

"If you're sure."

"I'm sure." Dena scanned down the row of photos on the light box.

"Well, thanks again, and if you need some help again, don't hesitate to call."

Dena thought for a moment. Perhaps she could use Jamie as a subcontractor. "Jamie, maybe we could work out a deal. I've recently purchased property up north, and I want to oversee some renovations."

"Uh-huh."

Dena continued. "What I'm thinking is perhaps you could do some subcontracting for me."

"I'm all ears. What do you have in mind?"

"At this point, I'm just brainstorming. Why don't we schedule a meeting after I return from Savannah?"

"Sounds great. Call me; I'm flexible."

Dena ended her conversation with Jamie and began to dream. *I wonder if I could operate out of Squabbin Bay if I hired several freelancers.*

On the other hand, if I went down to one overseas assignment a month, I could still work my own business without having to balance other people's schedules. Or I could increase my workload in order to make certain my subs have enough work. Of course the danger there is if someone couldn't make it, I'd have to fill in. And do I really want all those headaches?

Dena stretched the kinks out of her neck. She had a six-hour drive ahead of her to think and pray on this. Right now she needed to finish her office work in order to get on the road at a decent hour.

৵

Dena turned the key off. The engine quit. Her body continued to vibrate. She opened the door and took in a refreshing breath of salt air. Grabbing her overnight bag from the front passenger seat, she headed to the kitchen door. Inside, she found Wayne had put a fresh bouquet of brightly colored wildflowers. A note lay on the table.

> *Hope you had a good trip. There's some fresh*
> *fruit in the fridge, and I cooked and cleaned the*
> *lobster for you. I'm looking forward to your special*
> *omelet and, most importantly, your company.*
>
> > *Your friend,*
> > *Wayne*

The note glided back down to the table. She went to the refrigerator and checked out the supplies. Fresh strawberries and whipped cream were arranged on a small plate and a simple one-word note lay across the top. *Enjoy.*

Dena pulled out the small platter, reached for a strawberry, and dipped it into the bowl of whipped cream. "Yum," she moaned. "I like your style, Wayne."

৵

The sun rose over the horizon as Wayne left the harbor and headed for the inlet where he kept his pots. The salt air invigorated him. He glanced up at Dena's cottage. The house stood dark, but her car was in the driveway. A smile rose on his face, then he set his mind back on his work. The sooner he got it done, the sooner he'd be able to spend some time with Dena. It still boggled his mind that she was willing to drive six hours one way just to spend a few moments with him.

He pulled up the trap and discovered another empty pot. Oddly, he'd gotten excited when his catch increased the last haul. But today he found the same old pattern, a lobster here and a lobster there. Half were too small, and he had to throw them back.

He dumped the last pot over the side and caught a glimpse of Dena's cottage from the corner of his eye. A warm glow emanated from a single light in the kitchen window. Wayne checked his wristwatch. Seven o'clock. *At least she got some sleep.*

Popping the throttle into gear, he sped back to the harbor. The boat sliced through the waves and made headway through the gentle surf. *Lord, I don't understand this lobstering problem. Why is someone stealing from us small-time guys? The large companies aren't noticing a drop at all. Did Dena actually see the poacher? I'm okay financially, but old Ben Costa and others will be hurting this winter if they don't have a good season. Of course, You know all about that, Lord. But I suspect it doesn't hurt to remind You every now and again.*

Wayne continued his prayers as he docked his boat. Then his prayers shifted toward Dena. *Lord, only You know what's happening between the two of us. Father, I admit I'm attracted to her; it's just that I'd given up on finding someone special in my life years ago. Why now?*

Wayne clapped the mud from his shoes on the exterior of the truck's door frame and climbed into the cab. He headed home to clean up.

Showered and dressed, he smelled like a new man. He grabbed the small gift bag sitting on his counter. Its fancy bow evidenced that he hadn't wrapped the item himself, but he hoped she'd appreciate the small gesture. He hesitated with the bag in midair. *Have I gone overboard, Lord? The fruit, the groceries, the prepared lobster? No, I was simply taking advantage of going to the grocery store for her and picking up some perishable items. It's not my fault that the strawberries were in season.* He paled. *What if she's allergic to strawberries?*

Knock it off, Kearns. If she is, she is. You didn't know, and you simply struck out.

His truck bounced down the various roads as he wove his way toward Dena's cottage. He swerved to avoid a large pothole and turned down the long driveway to Dena's. The ocean came into view as it melded with the rich blue sky. *Lord, I do love this view.*

He shifted his gaze to the back door of the cottage. *On the other hand, I enjoy that one just as much.* He cut the engine and jumped out the driver's door. "Hi."

ა

Dena couldn't believe she'd opened the door before Wayne had even parked the truck. "Hi," she returned his greeting. Her palms began to sweat. She rubbed them on her jeans. "Thanks for the food."

"You're welcome."

He ambled up to her with his left hand behind his back and a great smile on his face. *Lord, he's handsome. Help me keep my feet on the ground.* "Come in." She stepped back and gave him room to pass. She caught a glimpse of something purple, she thought.

He glanced at the small table. She'd arranged it with two simple place settings and crystal stemmed glasses. The cottage didn't offer much in the way of fancy dishes. "I haven't started the omelets yet. I didn't want them to dry out."

"No problem."

"Thanks for the strawberries; they were delicious."

His grin broadened. *It doesn't take much to please this man,* she mused. On the other hand, he'd gone out of his way to create a fine feast. "There's a few left if you'd like some," she offered.

"I'd love them."

Dena went to the refrigerator and pulled out the small tray. Instantly, he reached for one.

"You're not used to waiting so long to eat, are you?"

"Guilty as charged, I'm afraid. I've been up for three hours already."

"I'm so sorry. Let me cook those omelets."

"Dena." He reached for her wrist. The heat of his hand around her wrist radiated up her arm. "I'm fine. I can survive for a while longer."

A rush of longing to be wrapped in his arms coursed through her. *Where'd that come from, Lord?* She stepped back. He released his hold. "I don't mind, and to tell you the truth, I've nibbled on a piece or two of the lobster. There are fresh muffins in the basket under the linen napkin."

"I thought I smelled something good when I walked in— blueberry?"

"Yes, good nose." She turned her back to him and faced the small stove. "So, how was the lobstering this morning?" A pleasant conversation flowed between them as she made their breakfast.

When the omelets were done, she spun around with the hot frying pan. On the table at one of the place settings sat a shimmery purple gift bag with white and lavender tissue paper neatly sticking out. "What's this?"

"Oh, just a little something for you." He winked.

Who is this man? And how does he know the little things that say "special" to me? "I'm not sure what to say."

"Absolutely nothing. It's just something to remind you of Maine while you travel to Savannah. At least I hope you'll take him to Savannah."

She slid the omelets out of the pan and onto their respective plates. "Can I open it now?" She placed the warm pan on the counter.

Wayne grabbed a pot holder and stuck it under the pan. "Sure."

Feeling like a giddy schoolgirl, she reached into the tissue paper and felt something soft, furry. "A stuffed animal."

"You must be horrible at Christmastime."

"Oh, hush." She pulled out the small stuffed animal. "A puffin. He's adorable." The bird was native to Maine; its brightly colored beak made it quite recognizable. Years ago, she'd done a photo shoot on the aquatic bird for a national magazine.

Wayne pulled out his chair and sat down beside her. "I'm glad you like it."

She looked down at her plate. "We'd better eat while it's warm."

Wayne reached for her hand. "Let's pray."

Dena felt a rush of embarrassment warm her cheeks, and bowed her head.

"Father," Wayne led, "we thank You for this meal, and we ask Your guidance in our conversation and Your direction for our growing friendship. In Jesus' name, amen."

"Amen." Dena glanced up at Wayne. With each passing moment, she found more and more she liked about this man. The fact that he wanted the Lord to guide their budding relationship was a major plus in her book.

He cut his omelet with his fork and took a large bite. "Mmm," he moaned.

Dena smiled. She knew her own abilities to cook, and cook well, but it brought a certain satisfaction to hear Wayne appreciate it.

"This is wonderful. I've never had an omelet with this kind of sauce before. What is it?"

"Basically, it's a hollandaise sauce like you'd use with eggs Benedict. But I always felt it went well with lobster omelets."

"Well, I've never had it this way, and it's great." Wayne forked another morsel of his omelet.

"Thank you." Dena sampled her own cooking and cherished the wonderful New England flavor of this dish. "Do you have any questions regarding the darkroom plans?"

"Nope," he mumbled with his mouth full. He finished swallowing, wiped his mouth with his napkin, and continued. "I didn't see anything there that didn't make sense. I'm thinking you might want to section off that plumbing from the house, so if you're going to be gone for long periods of time in the winter or won't be using the darkroom, we could drain it so the pipes won't freeze. It will save on the heating bill not to have to heat that area of the house."

"Interesting. Let me mull that over."

"Okay. Oh, I spoke with Jess, and she loves the idea of staying with you while she searches for an apartment in the city."

"Great. It will give us a chance to get to know one another."

Wayne placed his fork on his plate and wiped his mouth once again. "Dena, I love the fact that you've gone out of your way so we can spend some time together but. . ." He paused.

Her heart raced. Had she done the right thing coming up, or had it been a mistake? It felt right at the time. How were they going to develop a relationship if they didn't spend time together?

"What I mean is, I'm flattered. I don't understand what's happening between us, but I don't want it to stop. I don't understand how we can have much of a relationship with you living in Boston and me in Maine but—"

"I know," Dena interrupted. "It doesn't make sense. It's driving me crazy, too. That's why I wanted to come up—to spend some time with you in person. Not on the phone, not about business—just some one-on-one time to get to know each other. Do you have e-mail?"

"Yes."

"Good. We can write while I'm away. Wayne, as you know, I'm going to be on the road most of the summer. My schedule is very full. It's normal, I guess. I'm committed. I can't get out of the various photo shoots. But my schedule isn't nearly so full in the fall."

"Are you always this busy?"

"I guess. I haven't really thought about it. Since the kids have been grown, I've kept busy taking assignments I didn't feel free to take when they were younger."

"I think I understand. I'm pretty busy with the two jobs, but a man has to do what a man has to do. Jess went to college and I needed to pay for it."

"I helped all three of mine get through college. They're all married now. It's amazing how fast children grow."

"Yup. I remember the first day Jess went off to kindergarten. I couldn't concentrate on anything that day. Now she's graduated from college and has a serious boyfriend, who I finally got to meet for all of thirty seconds at her graduation. I don't trust the guy, but Jess keeps saying I need to trust her and her decisions."

"Of course you do. But that doesn't stop you from getting down on your knees and praying for the Lord to remove those blinders on you, or both of you, whatever is the case. Don't tell anyone, but I've been known to make a wrong assumption on my children's behalf every now and again."

Wayne chuckled. "Who hasn't?"

"True."

"Dena, I like you, but can a relationship between us really work?"

eight

Over the next four weeks, Wayne found himself asking that same question over and over again. Dena had traveled to Savannah and was now across the ocean in Africa somewhere. Each night they exchanged e-mails. Jess had moved into Dena's condo, and he found himself visiting Boston twice in a month. He booted up his computer and set a tall glass of iced tea beside the keyboard. The air was thick with humidity. An evening breeze from the east helped cool the house. Upstairs in his bedroom, he had one small air conditioner that fit inside the window frame. The rest of the house was outfitted with ceiling fans.

The Fourth of July was days away, and the summer heat seemed awfully warm for this time of year. Wayne took a swig of his iced tea, wiped his brow, and clicked on his e-mail. Disappointment filled him as he looked at an empty e-mail box. *Where's Dena's e-mail?*

He rolled his chair back and walked over to the front window that looked out on the small fishing harbor below. He glanced at his watch. Eight thirty, which would put it at one thirty in the morning where Dena was. Either the e-mail got lost in cyberspace, held up in a cyber highway traffic jam, or she hadn't been able to send him one. She did say there would be times when she'd be out of contact.

Turning back to the computer, he marched over to it and sat back down. His fingers froze for a moment over the keyboard. He tapped out a brief message.

Hi, I'm assuming you were unable to connect. I trust all is well. I missed not seeing a letter from you tonight. Know that

I'm thinking and praying for you.

> *Love,*
> *Wayne*

He reread what he wrote. He'd never signed an e-mail to her with "love" in it before. His right forefinger stood poised over the DELETE key. Did he love her? Well, in one sense he did. But would she interpret that as romantic love?

He deleted the comma and paused. Gnawing his lower lip, he positioned his finger over another key and retyped his salutation.

> *In Christian Love,*
> *Wayne*

Letting out a slow breath, he thought about that statement. It was true. It was honest. He could send this. *But. . .* He hesitated.

Somehow, it seemed too formal, too distant. They were becoming good friends. They found they could talk with one another on a variety of subjects.

Wayne hit the DELETE key and removed the salutation. Then he typed another.

> *Love,*
> *Your friend, Wayne*

He rolled his chair back and stared at the computer screen. *Yes, that one fits.* Grabbing the mouse with his right hand, he clicked the SEND icon.

Was he really ready to take this relationship to the next level? In some ways, it had seemed so natural to type "love." He did love her, but there were so many obstacles in their relationship. Her life's work took her around the world. His left him stuck within a thirty-mile radius.

He got up and strode over to the front window and looked at the lights surrounding the harbor. She would be here for a week around the Fourth of July. They could discuss whether to go further with this relationship or stop it before either one of them went too far. He had to be pragmatic about this. He loved Maine. He loved his life. He loved lobstering. How could Dena Russell ever fit into such a small world?

She couldn't, he reasoned.

"Lord, how can we compromise here?"

A stray thought hit him. *Aren't you getting ahead of yourself, old man?*

The phone rang. Wayne shook off his foolish thoughts and answered. "Hello?"

આ

Dena stretched her stiff body, trying not to disturb her traveling companion on the airplane seat beside her. The plane was making its final approach into Logan airport. The trip to Côte-d'Ivoire had been truncated due to internal uprisings in the government there.

Strangely, she'd been pleased to learn she was going home sooner than anticipated. *The first order of business is a bath.* She'd left the bush in a hurry and had taken the first morning flight out of the country, from Abidjan, finally arriving in Paris. Normally, she would have taken a room there and unwound before returning home. But instead of her normal layover, she took the next flight back to Boston.

Dena swallowed and eased the pressure building up in her ears. She'd learned to bring cough drops to help with the process. They seemed to work better than chewing gum. The plane banked and headed for the one runway at Logan that made those who had never before flown into that airport feel certain the plane was going to crash into Boston Harbor.

She rolled her shoulders. Seven hours from Paris was a long flight, but not as long as some she'd taken over the years. "Home," she muttered. *My own shower and bed in less than an hour.*

The plane's wheels skidded on the tarmac, and the engines roared as they reversed to slow the large jet. Once they were stopped at the gate, a single chime sounded, and the cabin burst into activity. Dena grabbed her two carry-ons, which contained her photography equipment and a change of underwear, should her baggage get lost. She would not allow her cameras, film, and equipment out of her possession. And with all the new scanning equipment since 9/11, no film was safe—which made going digital a huge advantage. However, being in the bush with no electricity for two weeks made digital impractical at the same time.

The convenience of being able to take the "T" from the airport to her condo had been one of the deciding features when she first purchased the place eight years ago. Although lugging her suitcases through public transit wasn't something she enjoyed doing every day, it was more tolerable than paying the outrageous overnight parking fees at Logan, or any airport for that matter. Being single, living in the city, and having a job that took her out of town more days than not required certain adjustments, she reminded herself as she pulled her overburdened bag up through the doors to the subway car.

The air locks of the sliding doors exhaled, and the transit authority train pulled forward. Living in Maine year-round would present another set of obstacles, she pondered. Dena glanced out at the row of tenement houses that lined the tracks. An image of an early morning sunrise refracting off the water of the Atlantic skimmed through her mind. Maine had its advantages, too.

Dena sighed. *Should I spend more time up there, Lord? I know Jason thinks I ought to slow down, and it would be nice to enjoy the grandchildren more. . . .* Wayne's rugged face and cheerful smile came to mind. *And, there's him.*

The train stopped at State Street, where Dena switched from the blue line to the orange line. A few short minutes on the train and she'd be home. *Home. . .my own bed. It sounds so heavenly, Lord.* Dena leaned against a post and closed her eyes.

Thankfully, her apartment was less than half a block from the train station. Dena hiked up the slight hill and pressed the button for the lobby elevator in her building.

Loud music filled the hallway as she exited the elevator. "Great," she mumbled. School was out, and some teens decided it was time to play their music as loud as possible until their parents came home.

Dena fumbled for her keys and walked down the hallway to her apartment. The music grew louder the closer she came to her own place. Slipping her key in the lock, she flung the door open. "What's going on in here?"

❧

"Wayne."

"Dena?" Wayne couldn't believe his ears. "Where are you?"

"Home, in Boston."

"When did you arrive?" He sat down in his overstuffed chair by the bay window and toed off his shoes.

"Thirty minutes ago and, well, I. . ." Her voice wavered.

"What's the matter?"

"I think I blew it with Jess."

"Jess? What's going on?"

Dena went on to explain about her arrival and not being too happy to find the music blaring in her apartment. But that wasn't the worst of it. She'd found Jess and Trev wrapped in each other's arms on the sofa. She'd made it clear when Jess moved in that no men were allowed in the house if there was no one else around. "Needless to say, I blew my stack. Trevor pulled Jess by the hand and stormed out of the apartment. I'm sorry, Wayne. I'm short on sleep and—"

"It's not your fault. Jess knew your requirements. I knew this boy wasn't to be trusted."

"Wayne, they were only kissing. But I'm glad I came in when I did."

"Me, too." *Lord, help me get through to Jess before she makes a mistake she'll regret.* "Thanks for calling. I'll call her cell phone and see if I can reach her. Does she still have a place to stay with you, or do you want her to find a new place?"

"She and I will have to have a heart-to-heart before I can decide that."

"I understand. And, Dena—I'm sorry."

"They're young and in love. Sometimes that combination isn't very conducive to making the right choices."

"Jess knows better."

"I'm sure she does. But what concerns me is, she didn't know I was coming home early."

"Yeah." Wayne closed his eyes and prayed Jess and Trev hadn't allowed their emotions to rule over their brains. Wayne wanted to trust Jess. She insisted on it. But she had to stop making such foolish decisions if he were to completely trust her. "Let me call her."

"Okay. I'll talk with you later."

"Bye, and thanks for calling."

"You're welcome."

He tapped in his daughter's cell phone number and prayed she'd pick up.

"Hi, Dad. Did Mrs. Russell call you?"

Caller ID on cell phones was a blessing, sometimes. "Yes. What's going on, Jess?"

"I'm sorry, Dad. Trev just stopped by for a minute and well. . ."

"And your word no longer means anything?"

"No, I mean, I'm sorry. I'm so sorry, Dad. Trev and I weren't thinking." He could hear the tears in her voice.

"No, you weren't. Is he there with you right now?"

"Yes."

"Put him on, please."

A male voice cleared his throat. "Hello, sir."

Wayne pinched the bridge of his nose. He didn't think of himself as a "sir" at the moment. He just wanted to shake some sense into this kid. "Trevor, I'm not pleased with your actions or Jess's this evening."

"I know, sir. I'm sorry. It won't happen again. I pulled Jess out of the place before that woman kicked her out."

Wayne held back a chuckle. At least the kid was trying to protect his daughter, albeit with a stupid move. "Trev, Jess was wrong to let you into the apartment. She'd given her word. You were wrong for showing up there in the first place. You knew the rules."

"Yes, sir. I'm sorry. It won't happen again."

"Well then, I think you'd better march yourself back to Dena's and apologize to her for abusing her trust. She just returned from twelve hours of travel to come home to—"

Trev coughed. "You're right. We'll go over there. But if she—"

"If she has anything to say, you'll stand there and take it like a man. Do you understand?"

"Yes, sir."

"Good. Let me speak with Jess."

A momentary pause lapsed before Wayne heard his daughter's voice. "Daddy, we didn't—"

"Jess," he interrupted, "you're an adult now. You are responsible for your own actions. I'm trying to trust you, but you've been making some foolish decisions lately when it comes to Trev. If you two are going to develop a mature relationship with the Lord in the middle of it, you're going to need to start making some better decisions."

"You're right. It's just so hard to. . ."

"I know, sweetheart. You need to make this right with Dena. I don't know if she'll let you continue living there, though. That's something you'll have to work out with her."

Jess sniffled. "I understand."

"I told Trevor to take you back to Dena's and face her like a man. My suggestion is for you to do the same. Face the consequences of your actions, Jess. I know it's hard, but in the end it will help you make better choices in the future. Trust me on this one."

"Okay." Jess paused. "Daddy, where do I go if she says I can't stay there?"

Wayne wanted to say, *Come home where you belong*, but knew he couldn't do that. Jess was growing up. She needed to face her problems head-on. "You'll have to deal with that when the time comes."

"All right." She quickly said good-bye and hung up the phone.

Wayne got up from the chair and paced back and forth to the kitchen. Why was it so much easier when she was five? At five, he could be her rescuer. Now, he had to sit on the sidelines and pray she'd make the right decisions. "Lord, give her strength. Help her make the right choices and not fall into the same mistakes I made with her mother all those years ago. Please don't allow that scripture to be played out in her life that the sins of the father are passed down."

How was it that life moments could bring back life sins? God had forgiven him years ago, and most of the time he forgave himself. But when times like this popped up, he'd reflexively take his past back and worry about his daughter's future. "Why is that, Lord?"

He glanced up at the ceramic lobster clock that hung on his kitchen wall. Jess had made it for him while in the eighth grade. It was painted in blues, greens, and browns—not the typical red everyone associates with lobsters. Instead, she'd chosen to paint an uncooked lobster.

It was nine o'clock. He should be in bed if he was going to get up at four to lobster in the morning. But who could sleep? Would Jess call him back? Would Dena?

Wayne paced some more and fetched another tall glass of iced tea. He took it outside and sat on the front steps. "Lord," he prayed, "how is it that the two women I care most about are so many miles away?"

nine

The last thing Dena had wanted to deal with last night was a two-hour sit-down with Jess and Trev. Jess was a good kid. Wayne had done a marvelous job raising her, but like most young adults, she and Trevor didn't always think before acting.

Jess wouldn't be making the same mistake again, of that Dena was certain. The evening had almost been a replay of one ten years prior when she found her own daughter, Amber, locked in an embrace with her boyfriend—now husband.

After a relaxing time in the Jacuzzi, Dena managed to fall into peaceful sleep. The next morning she woke and scanned her room before getting out of bed. It doubled as an office. Her room was hardly what a woman would call a retreat, but it was functional.

Wasn't functional what she needed? Her mind drifted back to the rustic cottage in Maine. That was most definitely not functional. The small bedroom barely fit the bed, and the white Cape Cod curtains, fluffy comforter, ruffled pillow shams, and bed skirt added a distinctly feminine touch. The hand-forged iron candleholders she'd purchased from a local blacksmith added to the quaint atmosphere.

Dena scanned her Boston bedroom again. On her dresser were piles of receipts that needed to be filed. Rolls of film cluttered the room. The small desk bulged with paper, film, and prints. *No wonder I like it so much in Maine.* The humor of the situation didn't escape her.

Stretching, she rose from her bed and dressed in a casual pair of jeans and a simple white blouse. She needed some order in her life, and the only way to get it was to spend a massive amount of time organizing her room and separating her business section from her personal section. *A small, folding room divider would do nicely,* she decided.

The first order of the day was breakfast. She hadn't eaten since Paris and she was starved. "Morning," Dena said as she passed Jess in the hallway.

"Dena, I'm sorry again about last night."

"Shh, we've already gone over it. It's forgiven and in the past."

"Thanks." The young girl's face brightened with the electric smile she'd seen at the church fair.

"You're welcome. Now what's for breakfast?"

Jess's eyes widened. "Breakfast?"

"You know, the meal you start the day with."

"Ah, you haven't looked at a clock, have you?"

"No, why?"

Jess chuckled. "It's two o'clock in the afternoon."

"Oh. Well, maybe a brunch would be in order." *No wonder I'm starved.* Dena scoured the cabinets looking for something quick and easy. Somehow, premade soups and meals that just required adding water wouldn't cut it. She reached for her favorite Chinese food menu and called in an order, then went into her room to check her business phone messages.

❧

The doorbell rang for the third time. The first had been her brunch. The second was Trevor looking for Jess. *It's probably Jess,* she figured. *She forgot her key or something.* Dena marched to the door and opened it. "Wayne?"

"Hi. Is Jess here?"

"No, I don't think so. I've been in my room working. What's the matter?"

Wayne handed her a crumpled piece of paper. She opened it and examined it carefully. "A credit card bill?"

"Yup, for a new stereo. Jess didn't need a new stereo, and she certainly didn't have my permission to charge one on my account."

"Oh boy."

"Oh boy, is right. What do you make of this Trevor character?"

Dena opened the door wider and stepped back. "Come in. Make yourself comfortable."

"Jess has always been a levelheaded kid. I don't understand these changes in her behavior. I never would have thought she would disregard your wishes and allow a man in the apartment while you were away. And now this. I don't know what to make of it."

"Love." Dena sat down on the couch beside Wayne.

"What?"

"She's in love and making foolish choices. They both are. Tell me, did she have permission to use your credit card in the past?"

"Of course. I gave her a card for emergencies. Personally, I don't see the purchase of a stereo as an emergency, do you?"

"Of course not, but I'm no longer twenty-two."

Wayne leaned the back of his head against the wall. He let out an exasperated huff. "I thought this parenting stuff got easier once they were grown and out of the house."

Dena chuckled. "One would hope. Actually, a year or two after college, it does ease up some. I still worry about all three of mine. Once you add the grandchildren to the mix—well, it's a never-ending cycle."

"I'm beginning to see that. Somehow, I did expect it to be easier by this point."

Dena patted his shoulder. "It will be."

"So, do you really think those two are in love?"

"Oh yeah. All the classic signs are there. They're so caught up with themselves, they forget what used to be normal for them. I once caught Amber and David in a similar position when I came home from an afternoon at the studio."

"Obviously, you didn't strangle them." Wayne winked.

"Obviously, or I wouldn't have those adorable grandchildren now. Seriously, I was much harder on Amber than I was on

Jess. She's a guest in my home. I'm hardly her parent and—"

Wayne held up his hand. "I already gave last night over to the Lord and to whatever decisions you made during your conversation with them."

"We reached an agreement. I think I helped her understand how to not give in to those impulsive responses, but only time will tell." Dena picked up the credit card bill. "This is another matter, though."

"Yeah. It's not that I can't afford the item; it's the principle of not asking and just assuming I'd pay for it."

"Why should you?"

Wayne knitted his eyebrows. His handsome green eyes held her captive for a moment.

Dena cleared her throat and tried to recall her own advice given to Jess last night. *Count to ten, pause, and slowly exhale.* "Don't pay the bill. Well, I mean you should pay it so that your credit isn't messed up, but you should make her pay you back."

"Trust me, she's going to pay for this purchase and any others."

Dena got up and walked across the room to the slider that opened to a very small terrace overlooking the Charles River. She heard his footfalls on the carpet following behind her.

"Dena," Wayne whispered, placing his hands on her shoulders, "I've missed you."

She turned and faced him. She reached up and glided a lock of his hair back into place. "I've missed you, too."

His fingers caressed the back of her neck. He lowered his head slowly. Dena closed her eyes. She wanted his kiss. She needed his kiss.

Somewhere in the back of her mind she heard something. She should pay attention to it—

"Daddy! What are you doing here?"

❧

Accepting a dinner invitation from Dena seemed the logical way to calm down after Jess admitted to having spent the money and didn't see what the big deal was about. Trevor needed a stereo, so she bought it. It was that simple. Well, not in his book. Since when did women start buying expensive gifts for their boyfriends? Weren't men supposed to do that? Had he been out of the dating game so long that the rules had changed?

"Earth to Wayne." Dena's voice broke through his muddled thoughts.

"I don't get it. I don't see what she sees in that boy."

Dena lifted the fork to her mouth and paused. "He's not that bad of a kid. He didn't ask for the stereo. It was just something Jess wanted to give him."

"I suppose. But still."

An edge of a smile rose. "You've got to face it; Jess made the mistake all on her own. Last night it was the two of them."

"True. But I don't like it any better. In fact, I think it bothers me more. At least if I thought she was being manipulated by the kid, it would make some sense."

"Perhaps, but you'd have another set of worries on your hand."

"True." He reached across the table and took her silky hand into his. "I'm sorry she barged in on us."

"She's a good kid, Wayne. She'll get through this period of adjustment."

He caressed the top of her hand with his thumb. "You avoided my comment."

"Which one?"

Most of the evening, she had skirted around the subject of their near kiss. "I want to kiss you."

"Not here," her voice squealed in a whisper.

"No, not here, but soon. I'm just putting you on notice." He winked.

She squirmed in her chair. "Excuse me." She placed the linen napkin down on the table beside her half-eaten dinner. "I need to visit the ladies' room."

That was smart, Kearns. What are you going to do for an encore? You know the lady is cautious.

Wayne drummed the table with his fingers. When she returned, he started to stand. She motioned for him to sit down and sat in the chair beside him.

"Wayne, I have to be totally honest with you." Her voice was so low he could barely make out the words. "I want to kiss you, too, but I'm terrified. Our relationship, as limited as it is, has awakened emotions in me that I thought were long dead. And they've come back with a vengeance. I need time to control these desires before we engage in anything more than holding hands. I know this sounds foolish but—"

"Shh." He started to place his finger upon her lips but then thought better of it. "I understand, and I can be patient. Please keep being honest with me, and I'll be praying for you. You can pray along the same lines for me, as well."

"It's a deal." She grinned and slipped back into her original seat.

"So, now that we've decided what we can't do in our relationship, why don't we discuss your next trip to Maine? When will you be able to come up?"

"Obviously, I have a week I hadn't planned on. But what's the shape of my cottage? Can I stay there while the remodeling is going on?"

Wayne eased back in his chair. "The progress is good, but you'll need to vacuum and dust real well before you stay there. I hooked up a plastic wall that has kept most of the sawdust from invading your living area. Although, come to think of it, you'll have to change your clothes in the kitchen. The plastic wall is clear, and with the bathroom and master bedroom walls removed, you—"

She held up her hand and crimson stained her cheeks. "I'll figure something out. I can shower at Jason's."

"I could find some black polyethylene. It would give you some privacy, but the black would absorb the heat and could make the house unbearable during the midday hours."

"No, don't bother, I'll work something out. Actually, I realized this morning that I have a lot of organizing I need to catch up on. My room is in organized chaos, if you can imagine."

"Actually, I can't. Your cottage is so neat, and from what I can see in your Boston condo, it's the same way."

Dena chuckled. "You haven't seen my bedroom." Again, her cheeks broke out into the shade of a dark pink rose.

"I'll take your word for it, but I find it hard to believe."

She laid her fork down on the table. "What I'm realizing is that I didn't make space for me. My bedroom doubles as my office. Since I gave up the studio and have been doing strictly freelance, my condo is also my workplace. I think that's what Jason has been trying to say—that my life revolved more around my work than around me, my family, and my relationship with the Lord. In Maine, my place has some nice feminine touches. Here, it's an office with a bed in it."

"Hmm." Wayne sat back. "I guess my dining room is my office. But my bedroom is simply a place to sleep. I've never thought of it in terms of a place to retreat."

"The rest of the house is always open for guests. But the bedroom, well, that's private, a place of solace. When Bill was alive, he and I often would retreat to the bedroom as our private place to just talk and unwind. After he died, the bedroom was my place to cry out to God in private. The kids were always welcome to come in, but, I don't know, it was where I did my devotionals, prayed my heart out, and tried to maintain some sort of sanity while raising three kids without a husband. Now my bedroom is, like I said before, an office with a bed in it. Nothing special."

Wayne nodded. He hadn't thought of his room as his private prayer closet to the Lord. It had been, but he hadn't thought of it in those terms before. "Interesting point."

Wayne's mind drifted back to more pressing matters. "What am I going to do with Jess?"

Dena reached over and squeezed his hand. He knew she understood. "Pray like crazy and trust God."

≥∙

Dena hadn't planned on another late night with Jess. But Jess needed an older woman to talk to.

Dena needed more time to grapple with her reemerging desires. Her body was waking up to things she'd once known and had long put to sleep with God's grace. Now she needed God's grace to get her through these early temptations and desires.

She walked over to her desk and sat down. Picking up a file folder, she began to sort and place items in their proper locations. If she couldn't sleep, at least she could get some work done.

"Ugh." She plopped the folder back down on her desk. This was exactly the problem—having her office in her bedroom. She went back to her bed, snuggled under the covers, and opened her Bible. Perhaps she'd find some relief in its words.

The next morning she found herself packing up the car and half of her paperwork. She was going to Maine, walls or no walls. She needed to spend time with Wayne and the building plans anyway, she reasoned.

Seven hours later, she drove up to her cottage and found Wayne loading his truck. "Hi. I thought you weren't going to come up."

"I thought so, too." Dena shut the car door.

"What's up?"

"You, me, these silly desires."

"They aren't silly."

"Okay, I'll give you that. But something has to be done about them. I can't live like this. And I figure the only way is to spend time with you and get over these initial—whatever these emotions are called. I can't have them. They're destroying my concentration."

Wayne smiled and walked up to her. He locked her in an

embrace that kept their bodies from touching completely, but close enough that she felt comfort in his arms. "I'm all for us spending more time together, but I'm not sure that's the answer."

"Are you imply—"

He cut her off. "They could get worse, more intense. On the other hand, we're two very mature adults and should be able to deal with them."

Dena took in a long, slow breath. "I hope so. My only other option is to never see you again."

He tenderly kissed the top of her head. "We can't have that. Come here." He led her by the hand to the tailgate of his truck and sat down beside her. He grasped her hands and started to pray. "Lord, You know our desires. You created them. Please give us the grace and strength to deal with them and rest peacefully in You. Amen."

"Amen. And thanks. We need to pray together more often."

"My pleasure. So, should I come back in a little while and bring some take-out?"

Dena smiled. "That would be wonderful. But how'd you like to strain those muscles of yours for a bit longer and help me lug this stuff in?" She popped the trunk open.

"Is this your entire office?"

"Nope, just half of what needs to be filed." She rummaged through the files and took out a large envelope. "I've been meaning to give these to you for a long time."

"What are they?"

"Open the envelope and see."

Wayne unfastened the metal clip then pulled out three large prints. "Oh, man. Dena, these are beautiful."

"I'm glad you like them. I figured with your recent concerns for Jess, they might give you a little comfort." She loved the pictures of Wayne and Jess together. Their love for one another was electric. Could her love for Wayne be just as powerful, if not more?

ten

Wayne wiped the sweat from his brow. The supports and frame of the addition were up. Today he was trying to box in with plywood the areas he could in order to give Dena some privacy.

He turned at the sound of a car driving up to the cottage. Pastor Russell and family were in tow. In a matter of seconds, the two children bounced out of the car and ran to the house calling out, "Grandma!"

Pastor Russell, dressed in jeans and a T-shirt, came over to him. "Hi, Wayne. Need a hand?"

Normally he wouldn't take a pastor up on such an offer, but for the sake of the pastor's mother's privacy, it made sense. "Sure, I'm trying to—"

The pastor held up his hand and cut him off. "I know; Mom called. I'll be right back." Wayne watched as the pastor lifted a cooler from his trunk and handed it to his wife. Then he pulled a hammer out of the trunk and came right over.

"Tell me where to begin."

Wayne decided the best way to go was to set the boards in place with a couple tack nails and let Pastor Russell follow behind and secure each board. The men worked until lunch, and Wayne was pleased with what they'd accomplished.

"So, this is where her darkroom will be?" Pastor Russell asked.

"Yup, and on the other side of this wall"—he pointed to an empty area—"she'll have her Jacuzzi."

Pastor Russell smiled. "I won't mind coming over to use that from time to time."

"Only if you promise to look after the place," Dena teased.

"Slave driver," the pastor teased right back.

"Leech," she said and winked.

"Why do you think I wanted you to move up here?"

Marie, Pastor Russell's wife, slapped him on the arm. "You're horrible."

Pastor Russell rubbed his arm. "She started it."

Marie rolled her eyes and Dena laughed. Wayne held back his own smirk. Then Dena's gaze fell upon his. "You should see us when all three of my children are here."

"Brace yourself," Marie warned.

"It is interesting seeing the pastor in a different light."

"Call me Jason, please."

Wayne nodded. He didn't think he could call his pastor by his first name. It seemed disrespectful, somehow.

Dena wrapped her arm around his, and her love filled him. It was a bold move for Dena to make in front of her son. It meant she was serious about developing their relationship. This warmed his heart even more.

"Come on, let's go eat before the kids polish off all the food." Dena tugged on his arm, encouraging him to follow her back inside the main part of the cottage.

Wayne washed up at the kitchen sink while the pastor washed up in the bathroom. Pastor Russell came out drying off his hands. "No wonder you wanted Wayne to have some help, Mom."

Dena blushed.

Marie cleared off the kids' dishes, and Billy eased over to his grandmother's side. "Grandma, Susie and I wanna have a sleepover. We wanna see the stars through the wall."

Dena chuckled. "Hmm, I might be able to arrange that. You'd have to ask your mom and dad, though."

"Please," the two children pleaded.

Pastor Russell cleared his throat. The children immediately silenced. "Seems to me your mother asked you to clean your rooms this morning before we left," he said in a stern voice.

Billy and Susie looked at each other. "We did."

"Did you have dinner plans with Wayne, Mom?"

The two children spun their heads back and forth between Wayne and Dena. Dena glanced over to him. As much as he would like another evening alone with Dena, grandchildren were a part of her life, also. "We could take them out for pizza."

"Pizza? All right!" yelped Billy.

Dena winked and mouthed a thank-you. "Sounds like I have some houseguests for the night."

"Yippee!"

Marie chuckled. "Go outside and play for a while," she encouraged the children. When they were gone, she turned to Dena. "Are you sure, Mom?"

"Of course. I don't get to spend much time with them."

"Well, I'll take them home for a couple of hours this afternoon and have them pack their stuff. That should give you a little break."

"Thanks, Mom. The kids will have a blast." Jason winked.

Dena laughed. "I'm sure they will. I'll be exhausted, but they'll do just fine."

The rest of the lunch was spent with some light banter and discussion about the renovations Wayne was making to the house. Then it was back to work. Pastor Russell stayed for another couple of hours and left with his family. Shortly after they left, Dena came to see Wayne in the new addition. "How's it going?"

"Fine. Your son helped a lot. You should have some real privacy."

"Thanks." She stepped closer. "Thanks also about the children."

"Not a problem. They're good kids."

Dena chuckled. "Sometimes."

She reached up and brushed some sawdust from his cheek. "You're quite handsome."

Shocked for a moment, he faltered with his response. "I think you're rather beautiful yourself. But if we keep talking along these lines, I'm going to kiss you."

Dena's eyes widened and she stepped back. "You're right. I'm sorry."

Wayne reached out and grasped her hand. "It's all right. Remember, we agreed we need to be honest with each other."

Dena looked down at the floor and nodded.

He curled his forefinger and lifted her chin. With every ounce of his being, he wanted to kiss her pale pink lips. But with everything that he stood for, he would not yield to that temptation. "Honey," he whispered. Her eyes sparkled with unshed tears. "Come here." He pulled her into himself and embraced her. "What's the matter?"

❧

Dena closed her eyes and relished his embrace. She felt secure in his arms. Oh, how she ached to be in this special place. For years she'd had no one to hold her except the Lord. And He had gotten her through some difficult moments. But, physically, she couldn't deny the desire to have this closeness with a man once again. How was it possible after all these years that she could find herself in this place? She wiped her eyes. "I'm sorry. I saw you standing there, with—well, we won't go there. Let's just say out of instinct, I wanted to kiss you, too. I don't mean to be cruel."

"Dena, I didn't find it cruel. I found it flattering, and, if I remember correctly, we mutually agreed not to go into a physical relationship at this point in time. That means I'm counting on you to hold me accountable, as I hope you'll allow me to remind you."

"You're right. Why is this so hard for me?"

Wayne leaned back against a sawhorse and crossed his feet at the ankles. "Because we've been there before, and, unlike most people today, we've kept ourselves from others for a long time."

Dena walked over to the hole that would one day be a window in her new bedroom and scanned the ocean. "You're right. And I want to kiss you. I'm just afraid."

"Like we agreed the other night, it's too soon. We can wait. And, Dena, you're worth the wait."

She turned to him and smiled. "You're a special man, Wayne. I love that about you."

"And you're a special woman, and I definitely love that about you. But we have even bigger problems than our attraction."

"What?"

"Our careers. Where we make our homes doesn't mesh very well."

"True. But the length of time between visits might help us."

"Perhaps. Sometimes I wonder if it isn't part of the problem. We don't see each other for a month and then—bam—we're together, and, well, the attraction is intense."

Dena took in a deep breath and eased it out slowly, then faced the ocean again. "You might be right, there. You know I'm leaving for another two weeks. Then I return for a day and fly right out again for another two weeks."

"Yeah, I know." He stood up straight and dusted off his backside from the sawhorse. "I guess I'd rather see you more often. But let's just say we get married one day. I don't mind telling you, I wouldn't want a wife who was only home one day a month."

"Ouch."

"Therein lies our real problem. Goodness knows, I'm attracted to you and even love many of the things about you, but I'm not sure where this relationship will end up. I keep questioning myself and God as to whether it's even wise to get this involved with each other."

"Double ouch."

"Sorry."

Dena gave him a halfhearted smile. "I've had some similar

discussions with the Lord. As I said, I'm fighting my head, my heart, and my body when it comes to our relationship. I'm as clueless as you."

"Where's that leave us?" Wayne walked up beside her and leaned out the window frame.

"Adrift on the ocean of love," she chimed.

"Oh, that's bad, really bad." Wayne laughed. "Seriously, should we stop this now?"

"Do you want to stop?"

"Not really. I'm hoping for a miracle, that maybe the Lord has something in mind that neither one of us is aware of at the moment. It seems odd that He'd put us together just to be friends, doesn't it?"

"Yeah, I don't feel this way toward my other male friends."

"Well, that's a relief." Wayne chuckled. "So, where are you going on these next two trips?"

"The Everglades, and then I'll be rafting down the Colorado River for a travel brochure. I get to feel the real adventure and travel with a team."

"Wow, I'd love to do something like that someday."

"Then, why don't you?"

"Work kinda keeps me busy."

"Year-round?"

"Well, yes and no. The income potential isn't all that high in this area, so one has to be frugal, and some of those adventure vacations can be pretty pricey. I have, however, gone white-water rafting here in Maine."

"Really?"

"Yup. But I generally go on a day run. Something I can drive up to and have someone drop my truck at the ending point."

"Do you use a canoe or kayak?"

"Canoe. I've thought about taking a longer trip and camping along the river, but I've worked hard for Jess to have a good college education. That doesn't leave much in the way of extra cash to play around with."

"Wayne." Dena placed her hand on his forearm. "You've given her that and so much more. You're a good father."

He placed his hand on hers. "Thanks, that means a lot."

Their gazes locked. Dena wanted to kiss him, wrap her arms around him, and pull him close. She blinked and stepped back. "Well, I better go prepare the house for the invasion of the grandchildren."

Wayne gave a halfhearted chuckle. "You're on your own after pizza."

"Chicken."

"Bock, ba-ba-bock," he crowed.

❧

Dena kissed Billy and Susie good night.

"Grandma?"

"Yes, Susie." Dena trailed her hands over the soft cotton comforter.

"Do you like Mr. Wayne?"

Oh boy. "Yes, honey. I think he's a nice man."

"I like him, too."

"Mommy said you might marry him," Billy chimed in.

Oh dear. "Well, I don't know if that's going to happen or not. We'll just have to wait and see, okay?"

"Okay." Billy nodded his head.

Dena straightened and stepped away from Susie's bed. "Grandma?"

"Yes, Susie."

"Would we call him Grandpa if you got married?"

Good grief. How do little ones come up with these things? "Honey, it's too soon to talk about such things. I like Mr. Wayne and—" *Goodness, how do you explain this to a five-year-old?* "We'll just have to see." She rubbed Susie's headful of blond curls.

"Okay."

That was easy, Dena mused.

She exited her bedroom, which the kids insisted on sleeping in because of there being no wall. She walked out to the deck and sat down, watching the starlight shimmer over the dark ocean.

Was it wrong to pursue a relationship in which you didn't know the outcome before you entered into it? Of course, who knows when they are going to fall in love with someone? Was she in love with Wayne? Was it worth possibly confusing the children, if she and Wayne couldn't work out their problems with career and locations? Perhaps it was best to end things with him now before she loved him too much.

Too much. . . That means I already love him. Dena groaned.

૨૰

Wayne delayed his arrival at Dena's, doing odd jobs that could have waited. He needed more time. He hadn't slept a wink last night. Instead, all he could think about was the impossibility of their relationship. He wanted to do more than kiss her. He wanted to make her his wife. He knew it was foolish to desire something so much, so quickly, while getting to know one another. After all, love at first sight was for teens, not two grown adults with mileage. But he had found love, and he'd fallen hard. He knew he loved her, but he also knew his family and life were in this community. He'd never survive in a city. Being on the ocean every morning brought life to his veins. Oh, he knew how silly and trite that sounded, but it was a part of who he was, of that he was certain.

He'd seen her on the beach with her grandchildren while he pulled his pots. *Empty pots*, he amended. She waved. He waved back, but instead of feeling the joy that had been there a month before, his mind swam with confusion.

"Hi," she offered when he arrived at her back door.

"You're making this difficult." He placed his hands in his pockets.

She handed him a mug of hot coffee. "You didn't sleep either, huh?"

"Nope. It isn't working, is it?"

"Not really. There's attraction, and I like you, but you're right. There are more difficulties to our relationship than either one of us is ready to deal with at the moment. I can't give up my career, and you can't give up yours."

"Exactly. So, why does it feel like I've been hit in the gut with a four-by-four?"

"Because we do care about each other."

"Dena, I wish I could just close up shop and be with you, but that's not who I am. I live off the sea. I'm a part of a community. There are people who depend on me. I know that others can fill that void but—"

"But, you're not ready to give that up, and that's what it would take if you were to be a part of my world. I know, I know. I played the scenario over and over in my mind tons of times last night, too."

"This stinks."

"Yeah," she agreed.

"So, where does that leave us?" Wayne asked. He watched her move silently to the coffeepot and refill her mug.

"As friends?"

"Okay." Wayne extended his hand to shake on the matter.

She turned away. "I can't. I'm sorry."

Wayne placed the mug on her table. With every ounce of willpower, he opened the back door. "I understand."

&

As he worked through the day, he watched her pack her car. He didn't blame her. He'd probably do the same in her shoes. Besides, she had to get ready for her next trip.

"Wayne, e-mail me any questions you have about the addition. I'll be out of contact for a couple of days, but I should be able to connect every now and again. The first week out on the river, I'll be out of contact completely. The Rockies greatly interfere with cell phone service."

"No problem. I think I have everything under control."

"I'm sure you do. I'm sorry, Wayne. I would have liked to work this out."

"Me, too. But I think it's better now before we're in too deep."

"Agreed. Good-bye, and thanks for all the work you're doing on the place."

Wayne waved her off and attempted to swallow the huge lump in his throat.

❧

The next month Wayne found himself miserable. The night before she left, they had been ready to trust the Lord; the next morning, they broke it off because they couldn't see it working. *Quite a man of faith,* he chastised himself.

He even stopped going to church for the month. He couldn't face Dena's son. And seeing him pull into his driveway right now made him want to pretend not to be home. "May I come in?" Pastor Russell asked.

"Sure, come on in."

"Wayne, Mom told me what the two of you decided. Personally, I can't argue with the logic but—"

Wayne gave him a halfhearted grin. "But I should still be in church, I know."

Pastor Russell sat down on the stool by the breakfast nook. "Actually, that isn't what I was going to say, but you're right, you should be in church. I understand your hesitation in light of my connection with my mother, but your spiritual home is in that church."

"What did you want to say, then?"

eleven

Dena stubbed her toe on the corner of a suitcase as she lugged them from the train station. The past two shoots had been the worst of her entire life. And the last thing she wanted to do was face Wayne's daughter in her apartment. She hoped Jess was out on a date with Trevor, a movie—anywhere but in her apartment.

She knew she'd been trying to live her own life and not listen to the many urges from the Lord to call Wayne and just talk with him. But if they were to only be friends, she didn't need to call him. After all, she barely called her other friends when she was on a shoot, she reasoned for the millionth time since leaving Maine. So, why did she ache to see him? To be held in his arms? Why hadn't those feelings disappeared by now? It had been a month. No one pines that long for a man they haven't even kissed.

Dena pushed the elevator button for her floor. When the doors opened, she paused for a moment to hear if music was again blaring from her apartment. A slight smile rose on her cheeks when she heard nothing, absolutely nothing. Just the way she liked it. Maybe she just needed to stay home for a few more days and unwind. Maybe rafting down the Colorado wasn't the ideal place to relax. Right—and elephants are purple with pink polka dots. *Face it, Dena, you love him, you miss him, and life is miserable without him.*

She unlocked the door to her apartment. The air smelled stale.

She dumped her luggage on the living room floor and found a note from Jess with her keys.

Dear Dena,

Thanks for the use of the place. I didn't get the job I wanted in Boston, so I moved back home. Dad says to call him when you return. Something about the addition. Thanks again for everything, especially our talks. They really helped.

Love,
Jessica

Dena picked up the phone and punched in the speed dial code for Wayne. She hadn't bothered to undo that feature. His answering machine picked up.

"Hi, Wayne. I got Jess's note. I'm home. Give me a call when you can. Bye."

She hung up the phone, and within seconds it rang. "Hello."

"Hey, Mom, just get in?"

Dena never thought she'd be so disappointed to hear Chad's voice. "Hey back. Yes, I literally just got in. Where are you?"

"Hawaii."

"Rough life." Dena leaned against the counter.

"Yeah. But I can't complain. Weren't you on the Colorado River yesterday?"

"Touché. What's up?"

"Brianne's pregnant and not doing so well. I was wondering if you could take her over some chicken soup."

"Hold it. Brianne's pregnant?"

"Yeah, we would have told you sooner, but you've been hard to get ahold of the past couple weeks."

"True. So when's the baby due?"

"Mid-March."

"Congratulations, son." Dena toed off her shoes.

"Thanks. Seriously, Mom, she's really sick. I'm concerned."

"I'll run over after I take a shower. I'll pick up some of Mr. Wong's chicken soup. I don't have time to make my own. But I doubt she'll want to eat it, if she's as sick as you say."

"I know it's normal to be sick but—"

"It's your first; you'll get used to it." Dena paused. "Kinda."

"Thanks, Mom. I really appreciate it. I'm glad you're home."

"You're welcome."

"Well, I've got to go. I need to prepare my flight for departure to Japan."

"Bye; thanks for calling." Dena hung up the phone and stripped on her way to the shower. Another grandchild. She grinned. Her quiver was getting fuller.

The phone rang again as she stepped out of the shower. Wrapping herself in a towel, she answered.

"Hi, Mom."

"Amber, what's up?"

"Did you hear Chad's news?"

"Yes, and you're horrible to even mention it, if I hadn't. I'm going to Brianne's now and bring her some chicken soup." Dena fished out some clean clothes from her dresser drawers.

"I doubt she'll get it down. She's really sick, Mom." This was a strong statement, coming from Amber, a doctor's assistant.

"Hmm, coming from you, I'd say it's more than the norm."

"Definitely. The poor girl can barely get up without getting nauseous."

"Eww. Did her doctor prescribe anything?"

"Not yet, but she called him this morning."

"Good. How are the kids?"

"Fine, anxious to see Grandma. Will you be able to come up?"

"I don't know, sweetheart. I'll try. I'm off again in three days."

"Mommm." Amber dragged out her name. "You can't keep working like this. It's crazy."

"I know. I'm cutting back, honest."

"Yeah, right."

She couldn't blame Amber for not believing her. For years the kids had been trying to get her to slow down, yet it seemed she was busier than ever. More assignments were coming in. She was regularly booked months in advance.

Thankfully, she still had one month blocked out. "I have September off."

"Really? Can we come to your house in Maine for a visit? I'm assuming you'll be up there."

"Some of the time. The rest of the time I'll be in Boston."

"Great, well I won't keep you on the phone. I know you've got a ton to do. Not to mention that Brianne needs some TLC."

"Okay, I'll call you sometime tomorrow and touch base with you."

"Looking forward to it. Bye, Mom."

Dena hung up the phone. "They must smell that I'm home." She glanced over to her answering machine and saw there were fifteen messages. They could wait until she returned from Brianne's. Amber had been really sick during her pregnancies, and for her to say Brianne was really sick meant the poor girl was suffering.

Dena was dressed and in her car within twenty minutes. She placed an order for a quart of Mr. Wong's chicken noodle soup and picked it up on her way over to Brianne and Chad's apartment. Finding Brianne pale and weak, lying in her bed, tugged at her heartstrings. *Have I made myself too inaccessible?*

She spent the night at Brianne's and took her to the doctor the next morning. It was the least she could do.

Driving home after settling Brianne back into her own place, she again prayed for guidance. Her cell phone rang just as she entered the car garage at home. "Hello."

"Hi, Dena, it's Wayne. I tried to get you last evening at your home and finally decided to try your cell phone today."

"I'm sorry, Wayne. Brianne's pregnant and very ill. I was playing nursemaid for the evening. I got your message to call. What's up?"

"Zoning."

"Zoning?" Dena closed the car door with her hip.

"Yeah, they're afraid you'll be dumping dangerous chemicals

too close to the ocean, so they've halted the addition until you can prove the chemicals you use in film developing aren't a hazard to the community—most importantly, to the lobster industry."

"Ah, well, I don't have that information handy. Let me talk with a few friends and get back to you on it."

"No problem. Sorry for the delay."

There was a pregnant pause between them. Leaning up against the garage wall, afraid to break the connection of the cell phone by entering the elevator, Dena asked, "How's Jess?"

"She's fine, but a little depressed that things didn't come together in Boston. But even more depressed that Trevor hasn't moved to Maine."

I can imagine. She held back the words of her heart. "Are there any other opportunities for her down here? She's more than welcome to stay at my place and continue her search."

"I'll let her know. Truthfully, I'm a wee bit concerned. A month ago she was making foolish decisions because of her overconfidence. Now she's not making any decisions."

"You got your baby back, but it's not the same, is it?"

"Nope, and I don't know why."

"Because she's changed. You've changed. You need to keep encouraging her to go out and face the world."

"Yeah, but it's. . ." He cut himself off.

"It's nice to watch over her once again. I know. Been there, done that. Hardest thing is to push them back out of the nest. Even if you don't have her leave the house, you at least have to get her out there in Squabbin Bay and working for a living."

"I know you're right. And she and I had that very same talk a couple of days ago. I still don't like it."

Dena chuckled. "Who does?"

❧

It had felt good talking with Dena about Jess once again. But as he hauled another empty pot out of the ocean this morning, his frustration grew. He'd never known a season as bad as this. And he couldn't understand why the poachers hadn't been caught yet.

He threw off his work gloves and grabbed his cell phone from the little cubby on the dash that kept it dry while he was on the ocean and looked at the reception. *Two bars; not too bad.* He dialed Dena's number.

"Hi, Dena, it's me, Wayne. I was wondering. . .could I hire you?"

"Wayne?" She yawned. "What?"

He went on to explain his idea of hiring her to stake out the bank by her cottage and photograph any and all fishermen pulling pots, specifically his pots.

"I'm willing to try."

"At least I'll have the evidence to prove my point to the Coast Guard. It's hard to believe the sheriff hasn't caught anyone yet. Everyone knows it has to be thieves. I've tried altering my times, and still I'm not catching much of anything." He placed one glove back on his left hand. "When can you come up?"

He heard some tapping as if a pen was being spun back and forth in her hand. "I guess I could come up late tonight. Chad will be home, so Brianne won't be alone."

"Brianne?" he asked.

"She's pregnant and very sick."

"Oh right, you mentioned that. Look, I hate to cut this short, but I'm on my cell. Leave a message and let me know when you can come and do the stakeout."

"You make it sound so cops-and-robberish."

"Well, it is. I need your help, Dena. You're the only person I know who has the telephoto equipment and wouldn't look conspicuous using it, especially from your own property."

"True. Okay, I'll get back with you. I just want to make certain Brianne's okay."

"No problem. I understand, and thanks. I really appreciate this. By the way, how much do you charge?"

Dena laughed. "We'll barter on it. I have some new ideas I'd like to explore with the addition."

"Hmm. I'd better end this conversation quickly before it costs me even more. Bye, Dena, and thanks."

"You're welcome. Bye."

He closed his cell phone and glanced up at her cottage. The addition stood out like a sore thumb, but in the end it would blend well with the original structure, especially after they stained and painted the exterior.

He scanned the ocean for any traces of the poachers. A distant roar of an engine caught his senses. *Should I?* He set the boat in motion and headed in the general direction of the remote sound. He knew most of the lobstermen in the area. Surely he'd be able to recognize someone out of place. On the other hand, what would he do if he caught someone?

Wayne eased the throttle lever back. *This is foolishness.* He turned back toward the harbor and prayed once again that justice would be found for those who were victims of these thieves and that the thieves would be caught. *Soon,* he emphasized.

❧

Later on that evening, he fought the desire to purchase some perishable items for Dena's refrigerator. She had family in the area, and they could help or she could purchase her own. They had to learn to be just friends. *Isn't that what Pastor Russell had been preaching when he came calling?* Wayne tried to remember details of their conversation. He'd been right that Wayne had been skipping church because Dena's son was the pastor. And as much as he enjoyed Pastor Russell, he couldn't help but be reminded of Dena and what they could have had together if their schedules and lives would have allowed it.

He straightened up and locked the addition. The cabinets and sinks had been placed in the darkroom. All the fixtures were now in place in the master bath, which included her Jacuzzi. Brushing off the sawdust from his trousers, he opened the truck's door. His cell phone rang.

"Hi, Dad, it's me."

"Hi, Jess. What's up?"

"I just got a call from Dena. She said she's on her way and will be able to help you out tomorrow morning."

"Great, thanks."

There was a long pause. "Dad?"

"Hmm?"

"What are you two doing tomorrow?"

The fewer who knew the better. He didn't want Dena to feel any pressure in case these thieves were better organized than he suspected. "There're some things on her addition we need to go over." This was true, but hardly the reason she was coming to town.

"Daaaad!" Jess whined. "Are you two getting back together? You should, you know. You've been pretty near unbearable. What's the big deal? She has a career and so do you. Don't tons of couples work those things out?"

"Jessica Elizabeth, this is not your concern. Besides, we aren't getting back together, as you put it. We're simply working together on business matters."

"Whatever. Look, Dad, smell the coffee. You like her. You're miserable without her. So figure something out."

Wayne squeezed his eyes shut. His relationship with Dena was far more complicated than Jess understood, and he wasn't about to be lectured on the intricacies of love by his daughter. "Jess," he said, in that tone only she would understand the true meaning of.

"Oh, all right. But please stop moping around like you've lost your best friend."

She is my best friend, isn't she, Lord? "Fine." Changing the subject, he asked, "So, did you find a job?"

"No, but Trev is coming up this weekend."

"Did you look?"

"Yes, but I'm being particular. I don't want to just waitress after four years of college."

He couldn't blame her. "Okay, but soon you'll need some

income to hold you over until the right job comes along."

"I know, Daddy, and I plan on working any job if I have to."

"Great. Well, hopefully you won't have to. I'll see you later."

"Actually, I'm going out with Marsha and Randi. We're traveling up to Bangor tonight. I'm going to look through some business directories for possible jobs to apply for."

"That's my girl. Okay, have fun. Talk with you later."

"Bye, Dad. Oh, I forgot. Can I borrow forty bucks for dinner and the search?"

"Sure, you know where I keep the cash."

"Thanks. Bye, Daddy." He could hear the skipping up and down for joy in her voice.

Wayne wagged his head. He was so easy.

❧

Dena slapped the alarm. Four a.m. She pushed herself up off the bed and groaned as her body protested this early morning wake-up call. But she'd promised Wayne she'd be on the lookout. Dressing quickly, she grabbed her digital camera with the largest zoom lens she had from the kitchen table where she had set it up last night and walked in darkness to the edge of the cliff. Her pulse raced in anticipation as she walked stealthily through the brush. Not that anyone on the ocean could hear her up here.

She lay down on the ground and scanned the predawn horizon. It was August, and the air was a cool sixty-five degrees, not the stifling temperature it would be in Boston. It was dark enough that she couldn't see the water and could barely make out some of the small rock islands in the harbor. Dena rested her head on her left arm and listened for sounds of boat engines. The waves gently crashing on the rocky shoreline was all she could hear.

Dena yawned. Her eyelids closed then opened again. A seagull squawked. "Night goggles might help," she quipped. In Africa she had waited in the bush for just the right moment when the animals would stir. But for some reason, waiting on e bluff for possible poachers didn't carry the same excitement.

Maybe it had to do with the fact that she wasn't really
:rtain she could help. She had a vague idea where Wayne's
ots were. With the night option on the digital camera, she
oped she could be of some use to Wayne.

The roar of an engine cut the silence. Dena aimed her
amera toward the ocean. She eased her stance. "That's not
boat engine, that's a car." She turned to see what she could
nly assume was Wayne's truck pulling into her driveway with
is parking lights on.

She didn't know whether to be upset or happy for the
ompany.

"Dena, are you out here?"

"Over here."

He cautiously walked in the dark toward her. His silhouette
:emed larger as it cast a dark shadow in the dim light of the
:ars. "Hi. I brought some coffee." He handed her a warm
aper cup.

"Thanks."

"It's too early to see anything yet, isn't it?"

"Yup, but I wanted to be in place just in case something
appens."

"Good plan. Normally I'm arriving at the harbor about now,
etting the boat ready."

"Do all lobstermen fish this carly?"

"No, but because I also do carpentry work, I like to get the
obstering out of the way first."

Wayne lay down on the ground beside her and placed a pair
f binoculars in front of him.

❧

'our mornings later, nothing had happened yet. During the
laytime hours, they finalized some of the finishing touches
or the addition and dealt with the EPA regulations for the
lisposal of the chemical fixer and silver recovery. At night,
)ena stayed alone in the cottage. She ached to be with Wayne,

but she didn't feel right barging in on Jason and his family every night, either. So there she sat night after night, alone. All alone.

"Wayne?"

"Hmm," he mumbled.

"I've been thinking. We might have given up too soon."

He rolled on his side and faced her.

Taking in a deep breath, she continued. "I know my schedule is ridiculous but—"

He reached out to her. "Dena, I want you in my life. You've become my best friend, even though we've barely spent any time talking with each other this past month. I know last month we were saying we'd trust the Lord, and then an hour or so later we decided it wouldn't work. Where's our faith?"

"We both see lots of potential for a relationship, but neither one of us wants to get hurt."

"Yeah, so what's the answer? I can't stop thinking about you. I pray for you daily—actually many times during the day."

Dena giggled. "And I've been miserable. Just ask anyone who was on those shoots with me."

"Jess hasn't stopped complaining about my mood. So, like I said, where does that leave us?"

"Between a rock and a high place?" She pointed toward the ocean.

"Bad pun." He gently stroked the top of her hand with the ball of his thumb.

She moved her camera and inched toward him. Reaching out for his rugged face, she caressed him with her fingertips. "I've missed you."

He captured her fingers and kissed them ever so lightly. "I've missed you, too."

She wanted to kiss him. She knew he wanted to kiss her. After weeks of desire, she leaned forward and captured his lips with her own.

The putter of a boat engine rang in her ears.

twelve

Wayne savored their kiss for days. While Dena and he hadn't caught a glimpse of the thieves, they had finally walked through their first barrier—themselves. She was now in Phoenix and working on another project. But they talked every night.

He tapped out a brief e-mail to Dena, letting her know that he missed her and looked forward to her return. He also mentioned he was thinking of pulling his pots for the season and sitting it out. In some ways, lobstering just seemed more frustrating than profitable. The few lobsters he was bringing in didn't even cover gas and bait. He finished the e-mail, clicked SEND, and went to the living room to enjoy a quiet evening at home. Jess was out with Trevor, and he was free to read the latest Alton Gansky novel.

Settling in his chair, he cracked open the new spine. He opened to the first page and had read the first line when a loud horn blast thundered through the evening air. Tossing his book down on the coffee table, he listened carefully to the town fire alarm. Two long, then two short blasts, and the pattern repeated three times. He was in his truck by the third series. Twenty-two meant Tarpon Cove Road.

As a volunteer fireman, he always went out. Thankfully, the sleepy little town of Squabbin Bay rarely had any fires. Wayne and the fire truck arrived at Tarpon Cove Road from opposite directions. Letting the fire truck pass, he followed down the street. Only a few houses dotted the out-of-the-way road. "Lord, keep everyone safe."

His heart caught in his chest when he saw Ben Costa's roof in flames. He pulled onto the sidewalk and jumped out of his truck. Ben sat on his front lawn, coughing. Another neighbor sat beside him, wrapping his arm around the old man. "Are you okay, Ben?"

Ben nodded yes. Wayne ran on toward the house. They needed to save as much of the home as possible.

Wayne worked with the other men for a couple of hours as they tried to save what they could of Ben's house. Pastor Russell came to the fire and added his hands to the work. Thirty men in all and two fire trucks came to fight the fire. The smell of wet, smoldering wood filled the air. Ben still sat on his front lawn as Wayne glanced back at the ruined structure. The house was an old wooden Victorian. Precious little could be saved.

With a bottled water in his hand, Wayne sat down beside Ben. "What happened?"

"I fell asleep in my chair while waiting for my dinner to cook."

"I'm sorry, Ben. Is there any way I can help you?"

"My kids been after me to sell the place and move in with them. Guess I'll be doing that now."

Wayne glanced back at the ruins. It had been a grand house in its day, but Ben's advanced years and the lean lobstering seasons of late had probably added to the building's tinderbox condition.

"I didn't know boiling water could burn a man's house down," he mumbled.

The hairs on the back of Wayne's neck rose. *First question, did he have a gas stove? Second question, what kind of pan did he use? Third question, how could a pan of boiling water ignite this large of a blaze?* "Let me talk with the chief, Ben." He gave him a comforting slap on the back. "I'll be right back."

Wayne walked over to Chief Emerson. "Hey, Buck. Any idea what started the fire?"

Buck removed his helmet and wiped his brow with a soiled handkerchief. "It's a strange one. Come here." The chief led him to the back of the house.

"See this?" He pointed to the scorched stones of the foundation.

Wayne nodded.

"And take a look at this." He led him toward the remaining walls of the kitchen. Wayne could see a pan still sat on the stove. Buck pointed in the opposite direction. "See that line? There was accelerant on these walls. Someone set the place on fire."

"Who?"

"That I don't know. But I'd say Squabbin Bay has a problem if someone's targeting old men in their homes."

Who would want to hurt Ben Costa? Did the person who set the fire even know it was Ben's house? "I'm going to take Ben home to my place tonight. He can call his daughter from there."

"Good idea. What did he tell you?"

Wayne filled Buck in on Ben's thoughts about how the fire started.

"So, whoever set the fire knew Ben was in there, unless I can find evidence of a timer. I'd guess they were in the house covering the kitchen wall with the accelerant while he was sleeping." Buck stepped back. "I need to talk with the sheriff. Excuse me."

Who would want to kill Ben?

Wayne called Jess from his cell.

"Hello," Jess answered.

"Jess, it's Dad. There's been a fire. I'm bringing Ben Costa home. Would you make up my bed with fresh sheets?"

"Sure. Is he okay?"

"Fine. He's going to be just fine." For tonight, he felt it best not to go into the details of the fire. "Thanks, sweetheart."

"You're welcome. By the way, Dena called."

"Thanks. Would you call her back and let her know what's happened? It's going to be awhile before I can come home."

"No problem. Talk to you later."

"Bye." He hung up his cell phone and rejoined Ben on the front lawn. The police were cordoning off the house with bright yellow plastic tape. The fire chief and sheriff were sitting with Ben, gently plying him with questions.

"Nope, don't have a problem with nobody, 'cept for them buggers stealing my lobsters."

"Have you caught someone taking your lobsters?" Sheriff McKean asked.

"Not yet, but I'm getting close. I can feel it in my bones. Their engine has a certain skip in the pistons. It's a very distinct sound. I've been listening. I know my hearin' ain't what it used to be, but I'm as certain as the nose on my face I'd know the sound of that engine if I heard it again."

So, had the poachers targeted Ben? Were they responsible for this?

੩৶

Dena rose long after the sun and headed for the bluff overlooking the ocean. There had been no evidence of the poachers coming before dawn on the mornings she and Wayne had been staked out between her assignments. Besides, she needed the couple extra hours of sleep after coming in late from her last photo shoot in Phoenix.

Her September vacation couldn't come soon enough. *I'll decide then what to do about future shoots and how busy I want my schedule to be.* With her mind decided, she scanned the horizon once again. Two days had gone by since she'd learned from Wayne that the fire at Ben Costa's was definitely arson, and that added a whole new level of seriousness to catching these poachers.

A boat nosed out beyond the peninsula that stuck out on the southern point. Dena aimed her camera and tried to zoom in on the bow and any markings on the vessel. It appeared to be similar to the other lobster boats in the area. Dena shot a few pictures, but the boat held its course out to sea.

A few more lobster boats and a couple of sailboats headed

out to sea from the north and the south of her position. But no one came to pull Wayne's pots, not even Wayne.

Okay, something's not adding up, Lord. If the harvest is so poor in the summer, why would someone steal now? Wouldn't they wait until winter? She decided she'd have to ask Wayne about that.

A small sailboat sailed into the bay. Its hull was wide, and the mast seemed to be more toward the bow than toward the center of the craft. Dena clicked off some more pictures. A couple of young people dove from the boat and swam in the bay. She watched them for a few moments, vicariously sharing the pleasure these young people enjoyed in a summer morning swim.

Deciding today would not prove productive in catching the poachers, she headed back to her cottage. The darkroom was finished, though the final touches on the exterior of the house and the bedroom carpeting had yet to be completed. Dena was very pleased with Wayne's work.

Her mind drifted back to the time she'd found him with his shirt off and working on the roof, his body well bronzed by the sun, his rugged features a feast for her eyes. As she stood looking at the spot where she had found him weeks ago, she caught herself drifting into unsafe territory. She shook her head and continued into the house.

In the bathroom, she freshened up for the day and discovered her roots were showing. She reached for her touch-up dye and applied it to the roots. Weeks on remote shoots were lousy for keeping up her blond hair. She had no idea what her real color was anymore. As she approached thirty, her hair started darkening, and as time passed, she started to rely more and more on a bottle.

With a towel around her neck and tinfoil wrapped around her roots, she glanced at her wristwatch and proceeded to the kitchen to make herself some breakfast.

She rounded the corner and screamed, then ran back into the bathroom.

"Dena, it's me, Wayne," he called from behind the closed door.

Wayne standing in the kitchen had not been what she expected to see. "I know it's you. What are you doing here?"

"I came to work. I didn't mean to scare you. Come out, please."

"No." *Okay, call it vanity, Lord, but I don't want him to see me with my hair like this.*

"No? What's the matter?"

"Nothing."

"Dena, for pity's sake, please come out."

"Later. I'm washing my hair."

"Honey, I saw your hair. I know that you're dyeing it. Come on out."

Heat blazed across her cheeks. "Wayne," she whined, "give a gal some dignity."

His laughter only flustered her more, but she wasn't certain why. Was she upset with herself for being so silly? Was she frustrated with him because he knew she dyed her hair? Or was she upset simply because she had been caught dyeing— with tinfoil in her hair, no less? In any case, she would not face him at this point in time.

"All right, I'll be in the master bedroom installing the light fixtures and ceiling fan. Come and get me when you're ready."

She didn't bother to answer him. She leaned against the bathroom door and slid to the floor. *He knows I dye my hair?* She groaned.

❧

Wayne whistled to stop himself from laughing at Dena's attempt to hide the fact that she colored her hair.

Standing on the stepladder, he pulled down the white, black, and red wires from the ceiling. He unscrewed the black plastic caps he'd placed on the wires earlier. Using his shoulder and head to brace the fan, he connected the proper wires to each screw and tightened them. Tucking the wires up into the hole, he attached the base of the fan to the ceiling. Once it was in place, he moved over to the other light fixtures in the master bathroom.

"Hi," Dena said. Her hair was still damp, but the renewed color shouted, "Hey there, notice me!"

"Hi." He stepped down from the ladder and met her halfway. "Sorry, I didn't mean to embarrass you."

A light rose blush swept across her cheeks. "No problem. So, what did you want to speak with me about?"

"Nothing. I just came in to say hello." He reached for her hands and marveled at their softness once again. "You're beautiful, Dena."

She released her hands from his and wrapped him in an embrace. "I've missed you, too."

He briefly captured her lips with his own then pulled back slightly. "You are beautiful, honey."

"Thanks. You're not so bad yourself." She tapped the end of his nose with her finger. "I have a question for you, totally off subject."

"What?"

"Something occurred to me as I was waiting to photograph potential thieves. It seems odd for people to steal in the summer if the lobsters bring less money at this time of year."

"Hmm." Wayne leaned against the stepladder. "That is an interesting point."

"It just doesn't seem to make much sense. I know there is some money in it, since the commercial lobstermen still fish. But if it's only the smaller operators like yourself and Ben Costa who are being hit this summer, why would they bother? I mean, wouldn't it make more sense to hit the larger companies, those with more pots, to earn more?"

"Again, you raise a good point." Wayne pondered this new information. She was right; it didn't make much sense, other than the fact that the thief still made off with a hundred or so lobster pots' worth of income. "I pulled my pots in for the season."

"I wondered, when I didn't see you out there this morning."

"It was simply too costly to keep it going."

"How long ago? Perhaps, if it's been enough days, the thieves won't be back."

"Hmm, hadn't thought of that. You're probably right. Ben has a few pots in this inlet still."

"I'll try again to get a shot of them if they should come by, but I'm thinking it's more and more likely that you've seen the last of them."

"Until I put my pots out again in November," he quipped, then shifted his weight and stood. "So, how long are you here for?" Something inside him longed for her to say forever, but he knew that wouldn't be happening.

"Five days."

"Wow, what happened to give you this big of a break?"

"I gave an assignment away."

He walked back over to her. "Dena, can you afford it?"

"I don't believe I have an option. I'm tired, Wayne, really tired. This commuting is hard on me."

He embraced her and encouraged her to lay her head on his shoulder. "Honey, maybe I can schedule time off the next break you have and drive down to Boston. What do you think?"

She lifted her head. "Are you serious?"

"Yes. It hardly seems fair for you to do all the traveling. If I'm not lobstering, I can rearrange the jobs a bit. So, when is your next turnaround time?"

They made their plans for the next visit then went back to their individual tasks for the day. Dena paid a visit to her son and grandchildren while Wayne finished up, getting the room ready for the next day's carpet delivery, then he returned home to prepare for their date.

Showered and shaved, he escorted Dena to dinner at a seafront shanty. It had plenty of texture for her photographer's eye, he hoped. But it also had some of the best seafood in the entire area. "What do you think?" He held her hand as they entered the small restaurant.

"It's charming, in a rustic kind of way."

"I thought you might enjoy it." He led her through the door. His fingers touched the small of her back, and a wash of comfort filled him. How was it that with so little time together, he felt so at peace with Dena?

"I'm glad you're here for five days," he whispered into her ear.

"Me, too."

The waiter, who doubled as the host, led them to a table that sat in front of a large picture window overlooking the harbor. The tables and chairs were of heavy pine with a thick, clear varnish. Candles that doubled as mosquito repellent sat on each of the tables. Ice and water splashed into the Mason jar glasses as the waiter filled them.

"Trust me, the food is great," he reassured her.

"Wayne, this is nothing, trust me. I've been to places where you swat flies faster than you can breathe. I don't enjoy those places much, but I've been there."

Wayne chuckled then sobered. "You've been to so many places I've only dreamed about or watched on National Geographic television specials. I can't imagine."

She propped her elbows on the table and locked her fingers together. "You know, I was serious about you joining me sometime. I'd love to have you come along on a shoot."

"What would I do? We're not married, and it just wouldn't seem right for me to traipse around the country, or the world for that matter, just to be with you. Not that I'd mind being with you; it actually sounds quite wonderful, but—"

"You're rambling," she interrupted.

"Sorry." Wayne closed his eyes and reclined in the chair.

"Do you know how cute you are when you get flustered?"

He opened his eyes and smiled. "No, but I don't mind you telling me."

He enjoyed her laugh. "I know it's not a masculine thing to

do, following a woman around on her job, but I'd love for you to experience some of the magnificent creation God has made out there. Not that this area in Maine isn't a great wonder."

"You don't have to explain. I understand what you mean, and I'd like to travel some. But—"

The waiter approached. "Are you ready to order now?"

He hadn't even glanced at the menu. "What's tonight's special?"

"Lobster bisque and swordfish," the waiter replied.

"Hmm. Dena, what would you like?"

"I'm open to anything. You decide."

Wayne scanned the menu. "Let's start with some oyster chowder, the local fresh vegetable medley, wild rice, and swordfish."

The young waiter stepped away.

"Oysters?"

"Do you not like them?"

Dena waved off his defense. "I like oyster chowder."

thirteen

Dena stood at the rail of her back porch and looked over the star-covered heavens. Tonight's dinner with Wayne had been wonderful. They were stepping toward a more lasting relationship. When he was beside her, it had seemed perfectly natural to ask him to join her on a shoot. Now, thinking back on the evening, she wondered why she even made the suggestion. After all, they barely knew each other. Well, perhaps that wasn't quite true. They talked and talked every chance they got and sent e-mails whenever a phone call didn't work out. She probably knew him better than she knew Bill when they married.

Lord, it seems like ages since Bill and I were together, and yet he's still a part of me. When I think of the times we spent together, of raising the kids, the memories are so clear and vibrant. I'm fairly sure I love Wayne. But how's an old woman like me, who's been a widow for more years than she was married, going to be comfortable with a man around the house? And what do we do about our careers? Each of us has a strong desire to work. I know I gave some thought to opening a studio up here. My kids would love it. And I know I've given some thought to organizing a team of photographers to go out on shoots, allowing me to take a more managerial approach. But would I really be content to do that? There's been so much adventure in exploring the world.

Dena paused for a moment and listened to the gentle surf rolling up on shore.

You know, Lord, if You're responsible for bringing the two of us together, don't You think it would have been better if we had more compatible careers?

Dena crossed her arms and sat down on the lounge chair.

"Nice sky tonight," Wayne said, bringing out two tall glasses of iced tea.

"Yeah."

"What's the matter?"

Dena took in a deep breath and exhaled slowly. "I was just thinking about our careers. I could lessen my load. My kids would love it."

Wayne sat down on the lounge chair beside her. "Dena, honey, are you happy traveling so much?"

"Honestly?" *Am I?* she wondered. "I don't know. I guess it's why I took the next five days off. I needed a break."

"Look, I know the world is an exciting place to see, and I truly would love to see it. But is that what's most important to you?"

What is most important? "My family is naturally the most important part of my life. But, I'll be the first to admit, I've hardly seen them over the past four or five years. It's hard to see how fast Jason and Amber's kids are growing up. And sometimes I feel guilty for not being around more."

Wayne wrapped his arms around her shoulders. "Why don't you tell me how you think you could lessen your workload?"

"Actually, I don't know that it would lessen all that much, but the traveling part I could reduce." Dena went on to explain how she could run a studio, even from here. How she could sell prints of her photographs and circulate some of her older prints for possible publication. Then she told him about subcontracting to other photographers. "Basically, my name would be on the line. I'd earn a percentage of what the photographer would be paid from the clients who hired them to come out for a shoot. But I'd also be helping them get established as well as helping them organize and hopefully keep steady work."

He leaned back on the lounge chair. "I think we should pray about it. It sounds like both possibilities have merit, plus you'd have more time for your family."

"Yes, but it's not just my family I want more time with." She wiggled her eyebrows.

"Woman, you're good for a man's ego. I haven't had anyone wanting to spend time with me since Jess was a young teen."

She turned to face him and grasped his calloused hand. "I'm terrified," she admitted as much to herself as to him.

"You're not the only one. I'm excited about the prospect of possibly finding someone to spend the rest of my life with. But I'm nearly forty-two years old and rather set in my ways."

Dena laughed. "Honey, you aren't set until you've hit fifty, and even then there seem to be changes that keep coming."

"Hmm, you might have a point there. Must be 'cause you're older and wiser."

Dena hauled off and smacked him in the shoulder. "Hey, I don't look a day over thirty-nine."

"True, but I know better. I know your son, and he's in his early thirties," he teased.

"Ahh, guess I didn't need to dye those roots, huh?"

Wayne roared. "You were quite a sight. How often do you have to do that? I mean, tinfoil on your head kinda made you look like you belonged in a sci-fi movie."

She went to swat him again, but he was quicker this time. He captured her hands and pulled her close. Millimeters before their lips touched, he said, "I love you, Dena."

Her heart leapt in her chest. *I love you, too,* she admitted to herself, not allowing the words to form. Instead, she kissed him with an honest fervor that caused them both to pause.

Wayne got up and walked to the railing. "It's getting late. I better get going."

Dena wrapped her arms across her middle. "Yeah, you're probably right."

"Honey, I—"

"Shh. Your instincts are right, Wayne. Go home. I think we both have a lot of thinking to do."

"All right. I'll call you tomorrow night."

Dena remembered he'd told her earlier this evening he had a job a short distance away and that he probably wouldn't get home until nine tomorrow night. She didn't want to let him go but knew it was best. They both needed to get a handle on this after their confessions of love.

They said their good-byes and shared a chaste kiss when he exited the house. She leaned up against the closed door. "Dear Lord, have I missed hearing those words from a man that much?"

❧

Dena hadn't professed her love, but her kiss drove the truth home. He tossed and turned all night. The possibilities of Dena's career changing excited him. For the first time since he met her, he saw a genuine prospect of how they might manage to live together as husband and wife. His heart even beat double time thinking about traveling abroad with Dena. If he were to see the world, he'd love to have her at his side.

But as dawn approached, he had to ask himself one very important question. Was he excited because this was the right thing for her to do, or was he excited because this would allow him to stay in Squabbin Bay? Why did he want to stay in this small town so much? Shouldn't he be willing to uproot and move to a place more conducive to Dena's career? After all, wasn't it the twenty-first century? Weren't women's careers just as important as men's? And Dena was certainly old enough that she wouldn't be taking off years to raise children. She'd already done that. *And done it well*, he added.

He headed to the job with that driving question on his mind: Was he willing to give up his career for hers?

All day and during his entire drive home, he continued to turn over every thought that had kept him awake the night before. When he arrived home, he immediately called Dena. No answer.

The little red light on his answering machine blinked. He pressed the PLAY button.

"Hello, you have three messages," the automated message intoned. One was a hang up. One was a sales call for refinancing his mortgage, something he had no interest in doing since he only had a year left on his present payments. And the third was from Dena.

"Hi, Wayne. I'm sorry, but I had to leave town. Brianne is alone and feeling poorly. Her doctor is thinking of putting her in the hospital for a few days and keeping her on an IV. Please pray for her. I'll call you as soon as I'm able. Or you can call my cell. I'm sorry. I really intended to spend this week with you."

He immediately tapped in her cell phone number.

"Hey, Dad." The screen door slammed behind Jess.

He cupped the phone with his hand and said, "Hi."

"What's for supper?" she asked.

"Don't know. Fix something, please."

"Sure." She shrugged and ambled into the kitchen.

Dena's voice mail came on. "Hi, Dena, I'm sorry to hear about Brianne. Jess and I will be praying. Call me when you can. Love ya, bye."

"Brianne's sick again?" Jess leaned against the doorjamb.

"Yeah, it sounds serious. Dena said they were talking about putting her in the hospital."

"I'm sorry. Let Dena know Trev and I'll be praying."

Wayne nodded. "I'm going to shower. What are you making us for dinner?"

"I'll order pizza."

He chuckled, tossing his head from side to side. "You're going to make a great wife one day."

"Yup, I'll have all the take-out numbers memorized."

He waved her off and headed for his room. In the shower, he lathered up, getting rid of the sawdust and grit. The warm water sluiced down his back, relaxing his tired muscles.

You should go to her, a small voice nagged.

He stopped mid-lather and looked from side to side.

Should he go to Boston? Would she want him there? What had he been fussing about with himself all day but sacrifice? Couldn't he give Dena a couple days of moral support?

He scrubbed his hair, working up a rich crown of lather, and rinsed it off. Finishing his shower quickly, he dried off and packed an overnight bag.

"Jess," he hollered from his bedroom.

"Yeah, Dad?"

"I'm driving to Boston; make me a pot of coffee—please."

"Okay," she replied.

His cell phone rang. Seeing it was Dena's cell, he answered. "Hi, honey. How is she?"

"She's stabilizing. She's lost a lot of fluid."

"I'm so sorry. Where are you?"

"Brigham and Women's Hospital. It's not too far from my apartment."

"When did you get there?" he asked, stuffing some toiletries into his bag.

"Just before dinner. I'm sorry I can't spend more time with you."

"Shh, Brianne needs you. I'm packing right now. I'm coming down there, unless you don't want me to."

"You're more than welcome—but you don't have to," she whispered.

"Honey, I want to. I'll get a room in a hotel near the hospital."

"No way. You can stay at my place."

"No, Dena. I'd love to, but I don't think that's wise at this point in our relationship."

"Ah, you're probably right. Okay, you can stay at the kids apartment. Chad's flying in tonight. I finally reached him through his airline."

"Okay. I'll be leaving in an hour or so, so I won't be getting there until dawn."

"Honey, drive down in the morning. Get some sleep."

"Tell you what, I'll pray about it. I'm so awake right now, I don't think the drive would be that bad. But I might get a few hours down the highway and be ready to zonk out."

Dena giggled. "I know you. It's already past your bedtime. You will zonk out, as you put it."

"You're probably right. I'll have my supper and see how awake I'm feeling. If I decide to leave tonight, I promise to pull over and find a room if I get sleepy."

"All right. Call me once you decide. I have to leave the cell phone off while I'm in the hospital, but I'm checking every hour for messages from the kids."

"Does Pastor Russell know?"

"Yes, I called him before I left town."

"Good, he's probably got the church prayer chain going for Brianne."

"I hope so." Dena paused. "Wayne, I'm really concerned. There's a chance she might lose the baby."

"I'll be praying. Hang in there, honey. I'll be there as soon as I possibly can."

"Thanks. And, Wayne—I love you, too. I'm sorry I didn't tell you that last night."

A smile creased his face from ear to ear. "You did, just not with words."

❧

Dena worked the kinks out of the back of her neck as the smell of bacon on the food trays passed in the hallway. It had been a long night. While Chad visited with Brianne, she stayed in the waiting room to give them some privacy.

"Dena," Wayne called, barely above a whisper.

She ran to him and held on, grateful for the presence of the man she loved. For so long she'd had no one to hold on to but the Lord. Wayne's strong body gave her renewed strength. "Thanks for coming."

"You're welcome. How is she?"

"Fair. They want to do an ultrasound to check on the baby."

She turned and walked back to the window overlooking the parking lot. "I hate hospitals."

"Huh?"

"They remind me of the night Bill died. I can't help thinking about it when I'm in a hospital. The smells, the sounds—everything reminds me of that night. I've been trying to put it out of my mind so I can concentrate on Brianne."

"What happened, if you don't mind me asking?"

She turned and faced him with a sigh. "He lost control of the car, and we flipped over a couple of times, so they tell me. I don't remember the accident itself. The police said it was a combination of wet roads, tires with a little less tread than they should have had, and driving too fast for the weather. It was one of those roads you know real well if you live in the area—so much so that you have a false sense of security about just how fast you can travel. Bill wasn't speeding, just not going slow enough for the weather conditions."

"I'm sorry."

Dena clung to him one more time. "Thanks. I really don't think too much about it, except for when I'm in a hospital."

"I understand. Would you like to get something to eat?"

"Sure. I don't recall when I ate last."

"Not good. Lead me to the cafeteria. I've never had hospital food."

Dena looped her arm in his and led him down the hallway. "You know, you're adorable."

"Naturally, makes me more kissable."

"Hmm, speaking of which. . ." She leaned closer and kissed him on the cheek.

He stopped. "Not good enough. I've driven six hours. I want the full treatment. On the lips, dear." He winked.

"With pleasure," she obliged.

"Mom?"

fourteen

"Amber? I didn't see you." Dena's cheeks sported a nice hue of pink.

Reluctantly, Wayne took a step back.

"Obviously," Amber chided.

Wayne had never met Dena's daughter. He'd seen pictures but never had the pleasure. Did she know about Dena and him dating?

"Amber, this is Wayne. Wayne, this is my daughter, Amber."

"Hi, it's a pleasure to finally meet you." Wayne extended his hand.

Amber narrowed her gaze on him and slowly shook his hand. "You're Jess's father?"

"Yup. Have you met Jess?"

"Nope, only talked on the phone with her when she was staying with Mom." Amber turned toward her mother. "Mom, I think we need to talk."

Dena looped her arm around his and patted his upper arm. "Wayne and I were going to the cafeteria for something to eat. Would you like to join us? We could talk there."

"Uh," Amber stammered, "sure."

Okay, she didn't know about Dena and me. Lord, give me a calm spirit after driving six and a half hours on little sleep, he prayed.

Wayne offered to go through the cafeteria line for all of them. Dena hesitated but took him up on his offer. She and her daughter were in a deep discussion as he approached. He set the tray down on the table. "I'll be right back with our drinks." At the beverage counter, he poured their coffees, adding enough cream and sugar for Amber's taste. She seemed to enjoy it very sweet—more like coffee-flavored cream than a regular cup of coffee. Of course, he'd been drinking the stuff black for years. It was another thing he and Dena had in common.

He watched the two women carefully as he made his way back. Dena caught his glance and smiled. His steps surer, he sauntered up to the table. Whatever Amber's concerns, Dena had obviously dealt with them, at least to her satisfaction. "Here ya go, Amber. That was two heaping sugars and a quarter cup of cream, right?"

"Right, thanks."

"You're welcome."

He set Dena's cup in front of her and sat down beside her. "It's a fairly fresh pot," he offered, trying to make conversation. "At least, I think it is. It was nearly full and didn't smell bitter."

Dena reached over and placed her hand on his forearm. "Amber's going to use the cottage in Maine next week, unless it's a problem with the construction."

"Not a problem at all. I should have it finished this weekend."

"Mom's told me so much about the addition. I can't wait to see it."

"Squabbin Bay is a great place, if you like the slower pace." He reached over to the tray of assorted food and passed Dena her salad. "Some folks can't handle it."

Amber's gaze followed every movement he made. "I'd be happy to take your family out fishing one day."

Amber and Dena chuckled. "David gets green just thinking of the ocean."

"Oh, well, perhaps a fishing trip wouldn't be a good idea."

"Thanks for the offer." Amber finished her coffee and stood, straightening her white uniform. "Well, I'm going to say hello to Brianne, then I've got to get home. It was nice meeting you, Wayne."

After Amber left, he asked, "Does she work here?"

"No, she took the T straight from work."

"Ah, so, how shook up was she?"

Dena looked down at her lap. "Not too. She reminded me of something I said to her the first night I met you."

"Oh?" He paused. "Are you going to tell me?"

Dena lifted her gaze and locked with his own. "I made a comment about your eyes."

"Oh?"

Dena shifted in her chair.

"Well, I have always had a fascination with green eyes."

Wayne stifled a chuckle with a cough. "And how is it I never knew about this?"

"I've told you that I like your eyes."

"True, but you never specified that it was because they were green."

She straightened in her chair. "Well, you never asked."

"What other secrets do you have in that pretty little head of yours?"

"You'll find out." She paused and winked. "Eventually."

"So, did I pass the Amber test?"

"She's curious, but she's more curious because she found us kissing in a hospital hallway. Seems that isn't something her mother would do."

"In Amber's defense, I'd probably have to agree with her. After all, you did tell me you haven't dated since your husband passed away, so your kids as teens never saw you relating in an intimate way with someone of the opposite sex."

"You have a point there. But come on, I am human," Dena defended.

"No, you're not. You're Mom." Wayne snuggled up beside her. "To your kids, that is. To me, you're the most fascinating woman I've ever been with. I love you, Dena."

She set her fork down, her salad barely touched. "I love you, too."

"Why don't you visit Brianne one more time this morning,

and then I'll take you home so you can get some rest."

She closed her eyes and sighed. "I guess you're right. It's been a long couple of days."

"I'll take care of this," he said, pointing to her salad, "and meet you in the lobby."

"No, I want you to come with me. Chad and Brianne need to meet you, and it would be better for them to have a proper introduction as opposed to the way Amber met you."

"Ah, I see your point. Let me get a container for your salad."

She nodded, and he left her alone at the table. He knew she was terribly concerned for Brianne and the baby. *Lord, how can I help here? I mean, I know I can be of some moral support, but apart from that, I don't have a clue as to what to say, do, or anything.*

"May I have a container to bring home a salad?" he asked the older woman in the gray and white uniform sitting by the register.

"Coming right up." She reached under the counter and pulled up a foam dinner container.

"Thanks." As he made his way back to the table, he noticed how vulnerable Dena appeared. A smile creased her sad face as he came into her view. *Maybe I just need to be here, nothing more, nothing less.*

⁂

Hours later, Dena lay in bed, thinking over the day. Chad and Brianne hadn't been surprised to see Wayne. Obviously, Amber had forewarned them. Her cheeks warmed again at the thought of Amber's catching her kissing Wayne. Of course, it was Amber who had encouraged her to think about having a relationship again. What had bothered Amber wasn't that Dena was dating but that Dena had failed to mention that her "friendship" with Wayne had progressed to that point.

No doubt she'd already called Jason and informed him, as well. Dena pulled the covers up to her neck.

She woke up late the next morning. Throwing the covers off, she dressed and glanced at the mirror to straighten her hair, applied a light coat of foundation, and highlighted her eyelashes. Wayne spent the night in Chad and Brianne's apartment. He should be returning any minute now to take her back to the hospital.

The doorbell rang. She quickly turned and the room spun. She reached for the dresser to brace herself.

The chime of the doorbell rang again. She walked slowly toward the front door. "Hi," she said, opening the door for Wayne.

"Are you all right?"

"Fine," she lied, without meaning to. It was just the automatic response to give when someone asked. "Actually, I feel a little lightheaded."

"Did you eat?"

"No." *When was the last time I ate?* she asked herself.

"Dena, honey, sit down. Let me make you something to eat. You can't go nonstop and not refuel."

"I know. I've just been too busy or too nervous."

"I understand, but it's time to think of what's best for you and your family. They don't need someone else in the hospital suffering from dehydration and exhaustion." Wayne marched into the kitchen nook. She watched him through the half wall that served as a breakfast counter on the living room side. Inside the kitchen area, Wayne stopped at the sink.

"How'd you sleep?" she asked.

"All right. It's hard to get used to a strange bed. At least it is for me. You must be used to it with all the traveling you do."

Dena reclined on the sofa. There was something soothing about having Wayne working in her kitchen. "Sometimes I didn't have a bed. A sleeping bag on a cot served me most of the time. Once in a while, it was just the sleeping bag, but I'm at a point where I can insist on a cot as part of my expenses for remote locations. Of course, the natives who have to lug the supplies along would probably prefer not to have the added weight. But I figure if they want me alert and ready to take quality photographs, a good night's sleep is essential."

Wayne chuckled. "I'm having a hard time seeing you roughing it in a sleeping bag. Jess and I go camping and canoeing every year. I think I mentioned that before."

"Yes, when I was heading out on that white-water adventure."

"Right." Wayne's words came back muffled. "Where's your omelet pan?" He closed another cabinet door.

"I don't have one."

"Sure you do. I made an omelet here for Jess—"

"Jess's," they said in unison.

"In that case, you'll just have some fancy scrambled eggs."

"Sounds fine." She watched him go to work on his breakfast creation. "Wayne?" He shifted his weight onto his left leg and turned to face her. "Thanks for coming down. It means a lot."

"No problem. I can't stay too long, but I'll do what I can to help while I'm here."

"Let's just pray that Brianne and the baby are stable today."

"Amen." He whipped the eggs with a whisk.

Dena leaned her head back against the wall and closed her eyes. The next thing she was aware of was Wayne's tender words waking her senses. "Hey, sleepyhead. Breakfast is ready."

She stretched and made her way stiffly over to the breakfast counter. He set a plate full of eggs in front of her. "Ketchup?" he asked.

"Salsa, if you don't mind."

"Salsa? Is that Southwestern?"

Dena shrugged her shoulders. She couldn't remember where or when she'd first had salsa on her eggs. "Could be, but I've been served it in Colorado."

He retrieved a jar of the medium spicy salsa from her refrigerator. "I've seen some put Tabasco sauce on their eggs up here, but I never heard of salsa. I suppose it isn't much different."

"Wanna try some?"

"No, thanks. I never got used to having ketchup on my eggs, never mind something spicier."

"Chicken," she teased.

"Quite possibly. I'm not a fan of spicy hot foods. I can handle a little salsa, mild of course. Actually, my preference with eggs is no sauce at all. Just call me boring." He winked.

Dena chuckled. "You're anything but boring. I find you quite intriguing."

"Hmm, am I a man of mystery?" He scooted around the half wall and sat on a tall stool beside her.

"Hmm, I won't go that far."

He raised a hand to his chest. "Ah, my life is an open book."

"Groan."

"Yeah, that is a bad cliché. Let's pray." He clasped her hand with his and closed his eyes.

She watched for a moment. Beyond his handsome features, she noticed peacefulness in his countenance.

After breakfast they joined the rest of the family at the hospital, discovering that even Jason and his family had come down. They were all pleased to hear that Brianne had gone through the worst part, and she and the baby would be fine. Jason and the children would stay for a couple of days. Marie would stay for a week and oversee Brianne's home recovery time. Chad would be flying out in the morning, at Brianne's insistence. Amber would take over after Marie left if Brianne still needed some help.

And then it hit her. All the family plans did not include her because of her busy schedule. "Lord, I guess it's time for a major life change."

২৯

Wayne stretched getting out of his truck. A six-hour drive made a man stiff, but thankfully he was finally home. Dena's mood had changed shortly after the family had made their plans regarding Brianne's care. He loved how this family pulled together and supported each other. Dena had done a fine job raising her kids. But what had been bothering her? They never could grab a moment alone for him to ask the question. And pondering it for six hours made him all the more curious. Something was bothering her, and he wanted to know what it was.

He glanced up at the starlit sky. It was probably close to midnight. He'd left Boston at dinnertime. Dena had packed him some sandwiches and a couple of cold drinks.

The smell of cigar smoke hung in the air. Wayne turned and looked around. A small red glow lit up the area near his hedges. "Who's there?"

"It's me—Ben. I been here waitin' for you. Jess said you'd be getting home kinda late." The silhouette of Ben's thin frame came into view.

"Come in and I'll fix you a cup of coffee or something."

"Can't stay. I need to get back to my boat. But I've been hearing some interesting things on the waterfront." Ben walked toward Wayne.

"Such as?"

"Seems you started a trend. Most of the small-time guys are pulling their pots, like you."

Wayne couldn't blame them. He'd crunched the numbers, and it was costing more to go out and bait the traps than he was earning.

"How about yourself?"

"Nah, I ain't never pulled them before, except when the water was too warm and we got hit with a bad case of worms. 'Course those were the days of wood traps. These metal traps last forever, unless they don't have enough weights in 'em when a storm hits."

True, but that's not why he came so late in the night to speak to me. "What's really on your mind, Ben?"

He stepped closer and handed him a large, overstuffed envelope. "It ain't much, but if something happens to me, would you be sure to give these to my daughter?"

He couldn't fault the man for being nervous after his house had been torched, but if he really thought his life was in danger... "Ben, what else is going on?"

"Nothin' for certain, yet. But if I'm right, people are going to be mighty surprised when I catch 'em."

Wayne reached out and grabbed Ben's shoulder. "What are you not telling me, Ben?"

"I don't think my house was burned down because of the poaching."

"Okay, what have you heard?"

"Nothing, not a blasted thing. But something's fishy, and I've got a nose for fish. I've been snooping around and, well, there's..."

An explosion ripped through the air. Wayne dropped down to the ground. Ben fell beside him and clutched his chest.

"Daddy!" Jess cried.

"Call 911! And stay down," Wayne ordered.

fifteen

Dena had never felt so torn in all her life. Being in Long Island and working wasn't helping to take her mind off of Maine and her family. Brianne was recovering, and the kids were lending a hand. Wayne was fine, but Ben's boat exploding made her nervous. Who was out to get the old man? He seemed such a likable guy. Wayne was convinced it had something to do with the poachers. What bothered her was that he wasn't leaving the investigation to the authorities. He had taken a far too personal interest in finding Ben's would-be attackers. Ben had suffered a heart attack when the explosion woke up the tiny village of Squabbin Bay. Fortunately, it was minor, and his daughter came and got him from the hospital. Not taking no for an answer, she had wheeled him, fussin' and fumin', all the way to her car. Now Wayne had taken up where Ben left off in his investigation.

Fortunately or unfortunately—Dena wasn't sure—Ben hadn't shared everything he knew with Wayne. Her prayer was that he wouldn't learn anything further until after the police and Coast Guard had discovered the true nature of the crimes.

Dena zoomed in on a bluff and a young seagull edging his way out of the tall sea grass behind the photo shoot. Holding the camera perfectly still, she ignored the bead of sweat rolling down her forehead. *Click.*

"Dena? Dena?" Kenny called for her.

"Over here," she answered and stood from her squatting position. She wiped the sweat from her brow with a no-longer-white handkerchief. "What's up?"

"I need you to shoot some more publicity photos. The client insists we didn't have the lighting correct."

Dena rolled her eyes heavenward. There were advantages to photographing wildlife as opposed to actors and models who insisted they knew more about the light and angles of a shoot than the photographer. "I'll be right there." She gritted her teeth and reminded herself that she could do this. Tomorrow couldn't come soon enough. Nothing seemed to go right on this trip. From the moment she'd arrived, one problem after another developed. *Is it the shoot or just me?* she wondered.

Putting on her professional smile, she greeted the customer once again, listened to her suggestions, and did as instructed— all the while knowing these photographs would not be used.

An hour later she finished the new round of photographs and said her good-byes. She'd driven from Boston in her own car for this remote shoot on Long Island. She opened her car door to let out the hot air then dropped her camera cases and equipment in the rear seat and put down the top.

A whistle pierced the air. "Nice set of wheels, Dena. Photography must pay more than I thought," remarked a young man as he walked around the car. She recognized him as one of the gofers who'd worked on the set all day.

"After many years and saving all my pennies, I was able to purchase the car."

"No way. How long did it take?"

"Well, if you don't count the eleven years of raising my children, it took four years. I've had the car for five."

"No way," he repeated. "It looks in mint condition." He examined the rear of the car. "Guess you're right; it is an older model."

Dena chuckled. "Yeah. So are you thinking of becoming a photographer?"

"Nah, I'm going into motion pictures. That's where the real money is. Plus, I have connections."

"Well, I wish you much success. Just don't forget to give time to the Lord."

"Oh, man. You're one of those born-againers, aren't you?"

"Guilty. I was a preacher's wife and my oldest son is a pastor."

The young man, with orange-tinged hair, stuffed his hands in his pockets and looked down at the pavement.

"Are you all right?"

"Fine, just heard enough of that God stuff."

Okay, Lord, this is the last thing I want to do right now. But if You want me to witness to this boy, give me the words, Dena prayed. "I'm not sure what you've heard, but there are Christians in Hollywood making movies today."

"Yeah, but I want to make the box office success films. I want to rake in the big bucks."

"Well, then you don't want to be the photographer. You want to be the director or producer. But even those who earn the big bucks have to learn their craft and learn it well. I'm afraid your goal is just making money, not the joy of learning to do a job well and liking it. I can't imagine working all these years and not liking my job."

"You didn't look too happy today."

Guilty again. "I'll admit, it wasn't the most joyous of days for me, but I still enjoy the craft. Did you see me slip away and take some shots when no one was looking?"

"You did?"

"Yup. I came across a beautiful butterfly opening its wings while perched on a flower. I held the camera still until the light shifted slightly and got some good shots before it flew away. Then there was the baby seagull."

"Who you selling those pictures to?"

"No one, most likely. But I have a granddaughter who loves butterflies, and I'll put a picture or two in a book for her. Or I'll simply give her the photograph to play with."

"But?"

The obvious questions played across his forehead.

"What's your name?"

"Michael."

"Nice to meet you, Michael." Dena extended her hand. Others walked past and headed for their cars. "I take thousands of photographs in a year. Only a small fraction of those are marketable. Could this butterfly be a marketable product? Possibly, but that isn't why I took the picture. I took it because I enjoy taking pictures. I enjoy being able to capture a tiny fraction of what God's created and saving it for others to enjoy." Dena leaned against her car. "Money isn't the answer to all of life's problems. Don't get me wrong, I don't mind earning a comfortable living, but it isn't the only reason to work. You need to find out what is special to you. Success is doing what you love, doing it well, and keeping your head on straight as much as possible. God equips everyone with special gifts. Talk to Him and find out which ones He's given you.

"I've been blessed, no question about it. But there were times when the kids were teens when I didn't know from one day to the next if I'd earn enough to put food on the table. What I did know was that I was doing something I loved and, with God's help, providing for my family."

"What about your husband?"

"Bill died when Jason was thirteen."

"Sorry." He glanced back at her again. "Why was it not an enjoyable day for you today?"

"Several reasons. But I guess the main one is Brianne, my daughter-in-law, was in the hospital last week because she nearly lost her unborn child. If I hadn't agreed to this job weeks before, I would be home helping her."

"Man, your life isn't like this Mercedes, is it?"

Dena chuckled. "Depends on how you look at it. If you're looking at the fancy paint, leather interior, and the Mercedes logo suggesting wealth, you're right, it isn't my life. Now, if you look under the hood and look at all the years of hard work and engineering that went into making this fine machine then, yes, my life is like this car. God's investing years of research and development in me, and He's still working on me. When

I'm done, I'll have this fine exterior and a wonderfully crafted engine and I'll be fit for heaven and driving on the streets of gold."

Michael laughed. "You had to be a preacher's wife."

Dena smiled. "True, but Bill died nearly twenty years ago. I've learned a few things since then. Do you go to church?"

"Not really. I have some friends who do. They're like you, really into this God stuff. They've been trying to tell me for a long time that money isn't everything. But you know, when you live in a place like this and you see the superstars of sports and movies all the time, it's kinda hard not to want it."

"I'm sure. But watch them closely and find out what makes them truly happy. Most of the time, it's the love from their family, not the things they own. A rich man is a man who has a house full of love, even if it's a simple cottage." Dena's mind flashed back to Wayne. He truly was a rich man.

"God bless you, Michael. I hope you decide to find your true gifts and work within those."

"Uh, thanks. I think."

Dena placed her hand on the boy's shoulder. "Keep talking with your friends. Take care, Michael."

"Bye," he said with a wave.

She slipped behind the steering wheel and turned the key. Her cell phone rang.

❧

"Hey, honey, how was your day?"

"Strange."

Wayne paced the front porch of the bed-and-breakfast where Dena had rented a room. According to her schedule she should have been back from the shoot two hours ago. He was beginning to wonder if his surprise visit would be a surprise to him and not her.

"What happened? Are you still on the shoot?" He heard the wind in the background, so he was fairly certain she was in her car. He prayed she wasn't on the highway heading back home.

"Long day. Suffice it to say, I hope I don't have one like that again. I did have a rather interesting encounter with a young man after the shoot."

The little hairs on the back of Wayne's neck rose.

"He noticed my car." She went on to explain her encounter with Michael.

"Did you decide to come home early?"

"No, I'm too exhausted. I'm going to enjoy the night off and possibly spend the morning at the beach before heading home."

"Hmm, sounds wonderful."

"Wayne, I think I need some solitude time. I think the kids might be right about my work schedule. I am losing my joy for the constant travel. But it means a lot of decisions will need to be made. Like how I'm going to support myself, for one."

Wayne sat down on an old wooden sliding rocker. "Are you saying we can't see each other while you're sorting this out?"

"Oh goodness, no. That's not what I meant."

Relief washed over him.

"Honey, are you up for a visit?"

"What?" she squeaked.

"I'm at the bed-and-breakfast. I rented a room. I'm on the third floor. I think it was an attic room years ago." Wayne rubbed the back of his head where he'd banged it earlier while unpacking his suitcase.

"Are you really here?"

"Yes."

"And this is your first trip outside of New England?"

"Yes," he answered tentatively. *What is she driving at?*

"And you did this simply to visit me?"

"Yes. Dena. Is there a problem?"

"No, no. I'm flattered. Let's book another night and spend some real time together."

Wayne chuckled. "I'm glad you said that, because I booked us both for another night."

"Pretty sure of yourself, huh?"

"I was. But, woman, you've got me wondering. Seriously, how long before you get here? I'm going stir-crazy waiting for you."

"Sorry, give me another ten minutes; I should be there shortly."

"Great. I'll wait for you in the driveway."

Dena laughed. "See you in a few."

She hung up the phone, not waiting for a response from him. Wayne clicked his phone shut, leapt off the front porch, and headed for the driveway. His heart kicked into high gear when he saw her red Mercedes driving down the rutted pathway to the seafront home.

She coasted into a parking space. "You're a nut."

"Hope you like nuts." He winked.

She smiled. "Love them."

His heart skipped a beat. *Lord, I don't think I believe in long courtships.*

৯

Dena lay back on the beach blanket and looked up at the night sky. A light breeze passed over her. She couldn't believe how one day could have started out so poorly and ended so perfectly. Wayne lay on the blanket beside her. He had flown from Portland to New York and rented a car out to the point on Long Island.

"Beautiful night," he yawned.

She yawned in response. *How is it that always happens?* "I still can't believe you actually came all this way to see me."

He rolled to his side and rested his head on his hand, his elbow extended for balance. "Honey, I love spending time with you. Besides, I might just get to see the world this way."

Dena chuckled. "Did you apply for a passport?"

"Not yet, but I've been thinking about it. Of course, I'd need some passport photos. Do you happen to know of someone who could do them for me?"

"Very funny." She sat up on the blanket, tucking her knees to her chest and wrapping her arms around her ankles. "Wayne, are we moving too quickly?"

He sat up and rested his elbows around his knees. "You know, I've been wondering the same thing. There are moments when I think we're going too slow, and then there are moments when I sit back and realize we've only known each other for a summer."

She felt a deep sense of comfort when she was with Wayne. A comfort she'd not known for years. It frightened and excited her at the same time. "Bill and I were high school sweethearts. We dated for three years, then married when he started college."

Wayne reached down and picked up a handful of sand and let it sift through his fingers. "Dena, I don't know if I'm ready for marriage."

Marriage? How'd he get—Oh, right, my relationship with Bill. "I didn't mean to imply I was talking about us getting married. Just that Bill and I dated for quite a while."

"Not that I'm suggesting we get married, either, but don't you think the three years were in part because of how young the two of you were?"

"No question. And if we were to talk about marriage, I wouldn't suggest a three-year courtship."

"Phew," he whistled.

"Oh, stop." She pushed him over to his side. "What's the game plan for tomorrow?"

"I don't know." He brushed the sand off his left arm. "What do you suggest? I'd love to see more of the area, if that's possible. The beaches are so sandy, so different from Squabbin Bay."

"A lot of beaches have sand," she teased.

"Okay, smarty-pants. You know the world; what do you suggest?"

"Well, are you driving back with me or flying home?"

"Hmm, guess it all depends on the company." He leaned over and kissed her cheek. "Driving," he whispered.

A shiver of excitement traveled down her spine. "Then I suggest we do some sightseeing and spend tomorrow night someplace else. Tell me what you've heard about in New York and New England that interests you."

"Goodness, there are so many places I've read about. I'd love to see the Statue of Liberty."

"All right. It's the other end of the island, and then some, but well worth the trip. Why don't we drive over to the Jersey side and visit Ellis Island, as well?"

"I'd love to."

"When do you need to get home?" She hoped it wasn't tomorrow night.

"I can be away for three days, but today counts as the first one."

"Gotcha." She stood up and dusted herself off.

Wayne followed suit and picked up the blanket. "I'm at your disposal, Dena." He captured her hand in his. "Show me your world, please."

Dena's heart warmed. Perhaps a summer was enough time to know if you wanted to spend the rest of your life with a man. She firmed up her grip of his hand. "Only if you continue to show me yours. There's so much I've never seen in Maine."

"You're on."

They walked hand in hand up to the old Victorian bed-and-breakfast. A good-night kiss, and Dena found herself lying on her four-poster canopy bed. For the first time in two days, she scanned the room, absorbing every detail. It was no longer a room to spend the night in while she worked. It was a room in which she would need to make some serious decisions. *Should I sell my place in Boston and move up to Maine, like Jason suggested? Or do I want to keep my life the way it has been for the past five years?*

sixteen

Wayne rolled his shoulders as he drove Dena's car up I-95. Full of unspeakable emotions, he worked his way through the thinning traffic. Today had been wonderful. He'd seen the Statue of Liberty and Ellis Island many times since he was a kid—books, TV, news, and movies. They decided to spend tomorrow in Boston so she could keep an eye on Brianne.

Dena stirred. *She's an amazing woman, Lord.* He'd been tempted to pop the question today but held back. Impulsive decisions to marry weren't wise, he justified. The matter would take more time and prayer. They needed to see if they could work with her schedule.

Dena blinked her eyes open. "Hi," she yawned. Straightening up in her seat, she asked, "Where are we?"

"Not too far from Stockbridge."

"We're making good time." She picked up her cell phone and dialed. "Hi, Brianne, sorry for calling so late. How are you?"

She paused.

"I'm on my way home right now. Which is why I called. I was wondering if Wayne could spend the night in your spare room."

Another pause.

"Great, thanks." She clicked the phone off.

"You're impossible."

"No, I'm thrifty. I seriously can't see you paying over a hundred bucks for less than six hours' sleep. Besides," she yawned again, "this way I can sleep with a clear conscience."

Wayne chuckled, grabbed her hand, and kissed the top of it. "I love you."

"I love you, too," She yawned again.

139

"Go to sleep, woman, before your yawning makes me tired and you'll have to drive."

" 'Night." She stifled a yawn.

Wayne took a swig of his now-chilled coffee. The caffeine would help him stay awake for the next two hours.

He drove for another thirty minutes when his eyes started to close. Thankfully, his cell phone rang. "Hello," he whispered.

"Daddy, it's me, Jess. I'm so excited. I'm sorry for calling so late, but I just had to tell you before I bust. I told Trev, and we've been on the phone for two hours. I'm just so excited."

Wayne grinned, then his grin slipped at the thought of a two-hour long-distance bill. "Slow down; tell me what's so exciting."

"Why are you whispering?"

"I'm trying to not wake up Dena."

"Dad?" she croaked.

"She's asleep in the passenger seat," he explained.

"Oh, sorry."

He couldn't blame his daughter for holding him account-able, especially since he also held her accountable, but it still felt a bit odd.

"Daddy, you'll never guess what I found in the mail when I got home from work this evening."

"You won the lottery?" he teased.

Dena stretched and sat up in her seat. He cupped the mouthpiece and apologized. "Sorry."

"No problem. Why don't you pull over at the next rest area and I'll drive the rest of the way?"

Wayne nodded. Jess continued in his ear. "So, what do you think?"

Ugh, I missed her big news. "I'm sorry, honey, Dena just woke up. I missed what you said."

"I got the job in Boston. Isn't that great?"

"That's wonderful, sweetheart. Is this the one you wanted?

Didn't they hire someone else?"

"Yes, and yes. Apparently, things didn't work out. I'm so excited, Daddy, I could burst. Isn't this great news?"

"Yes, I'm very happy for you. When will you be starting your new job in Boston?" He added the last tidbit for Dena's benefit.

"Next week. I have to give the job here a week's notice."

"I'm really happy for you; that's exciting news. Where are you going to live?"

"Trev said his parents will let me stay with them until I find a place. But I was wondering if Dena would mind letting me rent the room at her place again. What do you think?"

"I think you should ask her." He handed Dena the phone.

Dena placed it to her ear and listened. "Sure, let's start with four hundred a month for your rent. You're free to use what little food I have in the cabinets, but like before, you'll have to supply most of your groceries because I won't be around too much. As you know, I'm planning on being in Maine all next month. Same ground rules, right? . . .Good. I'll make sure your room is ready for you. I'll send a key home with your dad. I'll be on the road when you move in."

Dena said, "You're welcome," and handed the phone back to him.

"Hey, Jess, looks like things are coming together for you."

"Yeah, I'm so excited I can't sleep."

"Well, try. I'll be home late tomorrow night. Earlier if I can."

"Don't worry about me, Dad. I have to work until closing tomorrow night. I probably won't be home until after midnight."

"All right, sweetheart. Spend some time with the Lord, and I'll see you tomorrow."

" 'Night, Daddy, and thank Dena again for me."

"Okay, 'night." He clicked off the phone. "She says thank you again."

Dena chuckled. "She's welcome again. I hope she knows what she's getting into. It can't be good that the company hired someone and fired them within a month or so."

"I know. I didn't want to say anything to spoil her night. I'll bring that up to her one-on-one."

"On the other hand, it's possible the other person just wasn't right for the position."

"True. We'll have to trust the Lord, won't we?" He winked. Hadn't that been some of what Dena had been teaching him all along about grown children?

Dena chuckled. "Yeah, I've heard that a time or two."

"Are you sure about driving some?" he asked.

"Sure. Are you getting sleepy?"

"I was. It's a good thing she called when she did. I think I was starting to nod off."

"In that case, pull over now. I'll drive," Dena insisted.

Wayne laughed. "I'm wide awake right now. I can make it to the next rest area or exit, whichever comes first."

"All right."

"Thanks for letting her rent the room. Are you sure four hundred is enough?"

"It's low, but it's still my place, with my rules, so I figure she'll feel more at home for a while. She'll want her own place soon."

"But she'll need to save up for it. I'm just worried she and Trevor will make a foolish decision."

"Trust her, Wayne. She's a good kid."

"Yeah, I know." A sign came into view marking an exit in two miles.

"Have they talked marriage?"

"I don't know. Jess hasn't mentioned it. He's still living at home. Not that she isn't, also, but I've heard her mention to him a couple of times that he should be looking for his own place. He's working regular hours and has a good job. He's just content to stay at home, and I think that concerns Jess."

"It would me, also. But it's tough out there these days. Rents are extremely high, and unless you can get a group of four to rent a place together, it's almost impossible to afford anything and have money left over for food."

He flicked the turn signal on and slowed down for the exit ramp. "Yeah. I'm so proud of her."

"It shows." She tapped him on the knee. "You're a good father, Wayne. You've done well."

"Thanks. It was hard being a single parent, especially the single parent of a child of the opposite sex."

Dena giggled. "Tell me about it. I had two sons and no male role model other than memories of their dad."

"At least you had that."

"True. Didn't Jess's mother ever want to be a part of her life?"

"Not really. I talked her out of an abortion, and that made it hard for her in the small town. I can't blame her for moving away for college and never returning. She still sends Jess a birthday card and various other cards around holidays, but she has never visited with her or asked Jess to come see her."

"That's rough."

He pulled into an all-night service station. "Wanna fill up while we're here?"

"How's the gas?"

"Half a tank."

"Nah, there's more than enough to get us home." Dena opened the passenger door and slipped out of her seat. She bent down and touched her toes. "Feels good to stretch."

He unfolded himself as he got out of the sports car. He had to admit, he liked driving her car more than driving his old truck. It handled the road like nothing he'd ever experienced before. Temptation had been great to kick it up and really test how well it handled the road, but the better part of wisdom won and he drove at respectable speeds.

"She's fun to drive, isn't she?" Dena asked.

"Yeah, it is. I was just thinking how I've never driven any-thing that hugged the road so well."

"You should see it when she's up at really high speeds." She wiggled her eyebrows.

"How fast?" He leaned against the car and reached out to hold her. She stepped into his embrace.

"A hundred and ten, once. But only for a few seconds. I was too scared to keep driving that fast. I was out west, where you are allowed to drive insanely fast. The highway is straight, flat, and you can see for miles."

"I've heard about those roads."

"Wanna drive them with me sometime?" She leaned into him and kissed him on the cheek, then pulled away just as fast and hopped into the driver's seat. "Come on, let's get going."

✿

Dena couldn't believe she'd gone so far as to suggest a lengthy road trip with Wayne. Were they ready to make such a commitment to each other? She questioned herself all the way home. She dropped him off at Chad's, giving him her key to their apartment. He'd stayed there before, so he knew the layout of the place.

At her own place, she adjusted the thermostat. While she was away, she had left her AC on but at a higher temperature. Enough to keep down the hot summer humidity but not enough to have her electric bill skyrocket. Having Jess rent a room would change her utility bills. Maybe four hundred a month wasn't high enough. On the other hand, she didn't pay a mortgage on the place any longer, and the kid needed a helping hand.

She stripped off her clothes and slipped under a warm shower. Her mind drifted back to the day she'd spent with Wayne. They had so much fun.

Finishing her shower, she dried off, dressed, and went to her darkroom. The nap in the car had left her wide awake. She placed the film in the darkroom and separated out her personal pictures with Wayne from the work-related ones.

She shut the door and put on the safelight. Taking a bottle opener, she popped open the metal canister that held the used film and set each roll into its own developing tank. Once done, she flipped on the regular lighting and grabbed her suitcase. She brought it into the laundry room and set a load in the machine, then went back to the darkroom.

She had developed a pattern of doing things over the years. She poured the chemicals in the proper pans then set up to make some contact prints. Normally, she'd go to bed and rest, finishing the process of selecting which shots to print and printing them. But tonight she wanted to print the ones of Wayne at the statue. Occasionally, she'd written articles to accompany her prints, and she felt there was a story in one of these pictures, if she had captured on film what he'd captured in her heart.

She worked for a couple of hours and developed some eight-by-tens of Wayne, making a close-up of his head shot with the background behind him. The contrast was incredible. The rough exterior of the lobsterman-slash-carpenter and the tear of joy, pride, and conviction in his eye, set against the backdrop of the statue were breathtaking.

The clock read four fifteen. She really should go to bed. She glanced at her computer then marched over and sat down. She tapped out a brief summary of her thoughts and went to bed.

The phone rang a moment after she fell asleep. Groaning, she reached over and answered. "Hello?"

"Dena?"

She yawned. "Wayne, what's the matter? Why are you calling me at. . ." She glanced over at the nightstand clock. "Oh dear. I'm sorry, honey. I overslept." The plan had been for her to pick him up at nine.

Wayne chuckled. "You didn't go right to sleep, did you?"

"Sorry."

"No problem. Do you need to sleep longer?"

"Probably, but I'll get dressed and pick you up in thirty minutes."

"Brianne said she could drive me over. She has some errands to run, and it won't be out of her way."

"All right. Thank Brianne for me. How's she feeling, by the way?"

"She's looking really good. A whole lot better than when I saw her the last time."

"Great. Okay, I'll see you soon. I'll make breakfast."

"Don't bother. I'll pick up something on the way over. How late did you stay up?"

"You don't want to know."

"Oh?"

"Four thirty."

"Ouch. I'll drive today."

Laughing, she answered, "Any excuse, huh?"

"You betcha. Love ya. See you soon."

"Love ya, too. Bye."

Dena threw the covers off and went to the kitchen and put on a pot of coffee. Of all the supplies she kept in the house while she was away, coffee was a mainstay. She kept a couple of unopened pounds on hand, along with several varieties of flavored coffee beans to be ground. Today she would not take the time to grind the beans. Instead, she popped the plastic lid off a can and measured the grounds into her coffeemaker.

The coffee set, she scurried back to the bedroom and dressed. She let the rich aroma of the brew filling the apartment draw her to the coffeemaker, where she poured herself a much-needed cup.

As she lifted the hot liquid to her lips, the doorbell rang. She set the coffee down on the counter and answered the door.

Wayne smiled and held out a white paper bag. Brianne grinned.

"Yum. Come on in. The coffee's ready." Dena rescued her abandoned mug and took her first sip.

"We arrived before her first cup."

"Ah," Wayne said and walked into the kitchen.

"How are you feeling, Brianne?"

"Good. Chad left this morning. He should be back tonight. The airline is putting him on a more local schedule, allowing him to come home almost every night."

"That's wonderful news." Dena took another sip of her coffee. The fuzz was beginning to lift from her brain.

"Why were you up so late?" Wayne poured himself and Brianne a cup of coffee, then set the bear claws on individual plates.

Dena yawned and stretched. "I was wide awake when I arrived so I decided to develop some pictures."

"Do you do this often?"

"Sometimes." She walked over to the table, carrying her plate and mug. Brianne and Wayne did likewise. Brianne left her items on the table and walked toward the bathroom.

"How'd you sleep?" she asked.

"Fine. I hit the bed and don't remember a thing. I woke up around eight. That's oversleeping, for me."

She bit into the bear claw. "These are wonderful, thank you."

Brianne came wandering back into the room. "These are amazing, Mom." In her hands were the pictures Dena printed last night.

"Let me see," Wayne asked, reaching out for the photos.

"If you'll agree, I'd like to send those in with an article. May I?" Dena asked.

Wayne shook his head no.

"No?"

"What?"

Dena and Brianne looked at him like he had two heads on his shoulders. "The picture is—is—too personal." He pushed the eight-by-tens away.

"Wayne, that's what makes them great photographs," Dena protested.

He knew she was right, but he wasn't about to publicly display a photo of himself with eyes full of tears. *Not this guy,* he resolved. "I don't want to discuss this further. I said I'm not interested."

Dena let out a loud sigh and sipped her coffee.

Brianne nibbled at her bear claw.

Wayne's right foot started to bounce up and down.

Another stiff minute passed before Dena cleared her throat. "Honey, before you say no, I mean a final no—I mean, allow me to show you something to see if that will change your mind. Please?"

Brianne's head bobbed back and forth from him to Dena as if she were watching a tennis match.

"Dena, I know I'm sounding unreasonable here but—"

She leaned over and placed her forefinger to his lips. "Shh. Just let me show you the other part before you completely decide against it."

He nodded his assent. There was nothing she could show him that would make him change his mind. He'd be the laughingstock of Squabbin Bay if folks saw him with a tear in his eye. Having Dena's son as his pastor guaranteed the picture would make the rounds. And that was something he just couldn't stomach, no matter what else she had to show him. He glanced over at the photograph of himself once again. *How humiliating.* At the same time, all the emotions he felt standing there at the base of the Statue of Liberty flooded back in.

"Thank you. I promise I won't bring it up again if you say no after what I show you."

"Uh-huh," he mumbled and filled his mouth with a huge bite of the sweet bear claw.

Brianne stood up from the table. "I've got to run, Mom. I'll call you later. Bye, Wayne."

"Bye. Thanks for the place to stay last night."

"No problem."

"I'll walk you to the elevator," Dena offered.

He knew she wanted to say something private, like it wasn't Brianne's fault for his ugly disposition. And she'd be right—it had nothing to do with Brianne and everything to do with Dena. How could she take such a photograph of him?

A moment later she walked back into the apartment. She stood beside him with her hands on her hips. "All right, what just happened here?"

"Nothing."

"Nothing?" she huffed then returned to her chair. "I've never seen you behave like this. What's going on here, Wayne? That's a perfectly good picture and worthy of printing. I don't understand your refusal."

"I have my reasons." *Pride comes before the fall, or something like that,* he recalled.

"Well, you keep your reasons to yourself until after I show you what I wrote."

"You write?"

"Occasionally I'll write a small piece to accompany a picture. I'm no Tom Clancy; a few choice words could cause people to look at the picture once again with a different eye, perhaps. I don't know."

She writes, Lord? How did I not know this? Here I am considering asking this woman to marry me, and I don't know something as basic as this.

Dena left the kitchen and returned with a piece of paper in hand. "It's rough, but it will give you the general idea of what I thought I should say."

Taking in a deep breath, he reached for the page and began to read. A fresh tear came to his eye. He began taking in short, gasping breaths then long, slow ones to calm down. He let the paper drift back to the table.

"You can use my picture," he mumbled and walked away.

He needed air. He needed space. He walked out of the apartment building, down the slight hill, and across the street to walk along the Charles River. Water always calmed him.

"She's good, Lord."

seventeen

Dena didn't know whether or not to be relieved by Wayne's change of heart about using his picture. In reality, she was more confused. "What caused him to react that way, Lord?"

The kitchen now cleaned, she switched the loads of laundry she'd put in the night before, then proceeded into the darkroom to look at her contacts from the shoot. She needed to do something. *Who knows how long Wayne is going to walk off steam? If that's what he's walking off. He's obviously upset, but I don't know if he is angry or what. More like betrayed,* she guessed.

The smells of the chemicals assailed her as she walked in. She noticed a pan filled with solution. Pulling on a pair of rubber gloves, she disposed of the chemical. It wasn't like her to leave the room in this shape. She scanned the area for any other item that seemed out of place.

"Dena," Wayne hollered.

She dropped the gloves in the sink and went out to the living room. "I think we need to talk." She approached him slowly and gestured for him to sit on the couch.

"I'm sorry. I wasn't expecting to see myself crying in a photograph. I felt betrayed. It's like, I felt safe enough with you to let down my guard a little and—boom—you wanted to expose it to the entire world. I'm not used to this, Dena. Have you often used your family as models for photographs?"

"No, not really. There's been a print or two, but not many. When they were younger, I'd hang their school pictures in my studio. I had the school contract, so it was my work." She was rambling a bit. "Wayne, I'm not sure why it bothered you. I mean, it's a beautiful, touching moment. I'm pleased with how well the photograph captured your emotions. That doesn't always happen."

"Dena, I don't know how to explain this other than to simply state it. I'm a man. Men don't cry, at least not in public. You were asking to let the entire world see me cry. Do you have any idea how hard that is for a man? For me?"

"I hadn't thought about that."

He leaned back and closed his eyes. "You're right. It's a powerful picture, and your words will make a strong statement."

"Thanks, but I don't have to publish the print. I promise to keep personal moments I capture on film between you and me private."

Wayne let out a nervous chuckle. "Honey, you don't have to check with me on every detail, but I would like to see any picture of me, or us, you want to sell or put on public display before it goes out."

"Fair enough. You'll have to sign a release for the photograph to be used anyway."

"Thanks. So, now that I've spoiled our last day together, how can we redeem some of it?"

"Well, I need to drive you up to the Portland airport so you can retrieve your car. What time do you want to be home?"

"I was planning on eleven or midnight."

She mentally calculated that he'd need four hours for travel from Portland up to Squabbin Bay. Which meant he'd have to leave Portland by seven—eight, at the latest.

"What would you like to do today?" she asked.

He leaned into her and kissed her on the end of her nose. "Show me your city. I'd like to see it through your eyes."

Okay, so he has flaws. He's male; he's human, she reasoned. *But who in their right mind wouldn't want to be with this handsome, green-eyed man?* "History or contemporary?"

"Huh?"

"Do your interests lie with history or with modern-day things?"

"I have a fairly healthy interest in history, but I have seen most of the historical markers in this city on school field trips with Jess."

"All right, we'll lean to your carpenter side and visit some of the architecture."

Wayne leaned against the door casing. "Actually, I was thinking in more practical terms. Where do you like to go? What do you like to do? Where do you like to eat? Those kinds of places. What do you think?"

You're getting kinda personal. "Sounds like a plan. We'll start with a little Brazilian restaurant that has the most wonderful hearts of palm salad."

"Nothing too funky, I hope?"

"Funky? Didn't that word go out of vogue before your time?"

Wayne laughed. "Things take a little longer to make their way to us Down Easterners, you know. Especially back when I was in high school. Today, it doesn't seem to take as long."

Dena grabbed her keys and purse from the counter and looped her arm through his. "Come on, time's a wasting. This place is definitely funky. And I *am* old enough to remember using that word."

They departed her apartment with humor. "Bamboa's is really a mix of Brazilian and French cuisine. There's a huge fish tank with wonderfully colored tropical fish. The decor is loud with all the rich colors you'd find in places in Brazil."

An hour and a half later, they emerged from Bamboa's. "You were right; it was an experience, and the food was great. Now where to?" Wayne asked.

"You know, I've been wondering that all through dinner. There are so many little places I like in the city, but they are not the kinds of places where you spend time, real time, with someone. Since it's going to be another week before we see each other, I was wondering if we could just spend some downtime together."

❧

Wayne sat back on his deck with a tall glass of iced tea. Dena would be arriving tomorrow for an entire month. The past ten days had been the longest in the history of mankind. At least in his history. They'd had such a good time together in New York and Boston, focusing on work seemed futile.

Jess was now living in Boston at Dena's apartment. How was it that in a few months his life had so radically changed?

His phone rang. "Hello," he answered.

"Hi, Wayne, I'm home."

"Hey, how was your trip?"

"Miserable. I missed you."

His heart took flight at those three simple words. "I missed you, too. How's Jess?"

"I haven't a clue. She appears to have moved in, but she's not here right now. I'm packing for the month. I managed to get a couple of bags packed before I left, but I need to do laundry tonight before I can come up tomorrow."

"The house is ready."

"Oh, honey, I appreciate that so much. I've been rethinking Jason's suggestion that I make Maine my residence. While I was away, Amber e-mailed me. She and David are really having a tough time. He's still not able to find work, and she's so busy working. Jason's been talking with David about some possible work in Maine. Amber could easily transfer as a nurse to a local hospital. It just seems my family needs me here."

His heart sank. He would have hoped she would have mentioned him in there somewhere. "I'll pray with you about it."

"Thanks. I appreciate it. Actually, to be totally honest, I'd like to spend more time with you, too. Is that possible?"

His heart leaped up and did a somersault. "I'd like that." He lowered his voice. "I love you, Dena."

"I love you, too. Any fears?"

"Tons, but we've been over that ground before. This next month will be a real test."

"Only way to find out is to just jump right in and live it."
Wayne grinned and fired a silent praise heavenward.

"Yeah, that's why I decided to move most of my lab and files with me."

"You're kidding! Are you serious?"

"Yes."

"Dena, you've really given this a lot of thought, haven't you?"

"I started thinking about this months ago, when I made the decision to have a darkroom put in the cottage. If I were conservative with my funds, I could live off of my investments now. But I enjoy working. I have to stay active. Is there really enough up there in Maine to keep me busy?"

"I don't know, Dena. That's always been my fear. You've traveled the world. You enjoy traveling, and here I sit in a very small town with a very boring life. How can I compete with your career?"

"If you say it that way, you can't. But there's something about being up there that recharges me. I'd like to think it's the Lord and having more time with Him, but I know it also has to do with a certain green-eyed man who lives up there."

Wayne sat down on the old rocker by the fireplace. He should be rejoicing, but something about the entire weight of the state of Maine sat on his shoulders. He couldn't be responsible for Dena giving up her career. There had to be another way. She was far too gifted of a photographer.

"Wayne?"

Her calling his name jarred him back to the phone call. "Sorry, I'm—" He rubbed the back of his neck. "I don't know what to say, Dena. I don't know what to do. I want you here, but something feels off. Are you sure? Absolutely sure?"

❧

Dena wasn't sure about anything. She'd been battling herself the entire week about whether or not she was making the right decision. And driving up the interstate hadn't confirmed her decision one way or the other. David and Amber were going to rent a truck and bring up the rest of Dena's belongings this weekend. Wayne's nervousness about her changing her career plans didn't help her concerns, either. Weren't they always talking around the subject of making their relationship more permanent? Hadn't their weekend ten days ago confirmed their desires to spend more time together? What was he afraid of?

Dena drummed her cherry red fingernails on the steering wheel. She took in a long breath and eased it out slowly. Hadn't she decided last week that the family needed her? Isn't that really why she was making this change? Brianne's health continued to be a concern.

Yes, the family needed her around—or she needed to be around her family more. In either case, it was the right decision even if nothing developed between her and Wayne.

Her cottage came into view. The ocean shimmered in the sunlight. She took in a deep breath of salt air. "Home," she sighed. "When did this cottage become my home instead of my apartment in Boston?"

She grabbed two bags from the trunk and headed inside. Dropping them on the kitchen floor, she walked back to the hallway entrance to the addition. For the first time, it wasn't covered in plastic. Slowly, she worked her way into the new section and traced the edges of the woodwork with her right forefinger. "You do excellent work, Wayne. Thank you."

The Jacuzzi in the master bathroom was her next stop. The room glistened. The carpet had been put in and looked wonderful next to the stone floor surrounding the hot tub. She looked up, and there she found a skylight directly overhead. She imagined herself late at night, unwinding after a long day of work in the darkroom, feeling the warmth of the hot jets on her back as she looked up at the sky, relaxing. Totally relaxing. "Calgon, take me away," she whispered.

The idea of jumping into the Jacuzzi flitted through her mind. Then reality hit: There were more bags and boxes to

unload. Not to mention that the house needed to cool down.
She switched on the central air before heading out to the car
for another load.

"Hi, Mom," Jason said with a box in his hand.

"How'd you know I was here?"

"Amber called. Besides, Jenny Thompson called when you
got off the interstate."

"Jenny Thompson?"

"She owns a place near the four corners in town."

"Ah, but how do I know her?"

"You don't, but she knows you."

"Jason, how do you stand it? I mean, with everyone knowing
everyone's business."

Jason shifted the weight of the box onto his hip. "Most folks
don't pay the gossip no never mind. But there is an upside
to the small community, and that's if you're in trouble, folks
are always there to lend a hand. And notice when you need a
hand," he added with a wink.

"I suppose Amber told you that I'm going to try living up
here on a more permanent basis."

"She did."

Dena pulled another box out of the trunk and led them
back into the house. "What do you think?"

"I think there's more to it than what you told Amber. Just
how serious are you and Wayne, Mom?"

eighteen

Wayne found Dena and Pastor Russell in deep conversation, and, by the startled stares he received, he could only assume he'd been the topic of discussion.

"I was wondering if you'd like to go out for dinner," he told Dena shortly after Pastor Russell left.

"Actually, I'm beat. But you're welcome to have dinner with me. Of course, it'll be some frozen dinner or something out of a can."

Wayne smiled. "I'll take what I can get. Or I could drive to town and pick up a couple of fresh steaks for the grill."

"Are you cooking?" she asked, grabbing a suitcase.

"Sure. I'll even pick up some corn on the cob and potato salad. How's that sound?"

"Wonderful. I'm starving."

Wayne chuckled. "Honey, when aren't you hungry?" he teased.

"Hey, I resemble that," she quipped.

"Oh?" He pulled her toward him. It had been ages since they had shared a kiss. Well, maybe not ages, but eleven days was long enough. The kiss lengthened, and he felt her tension melt in his arms along with his own. He hadn't been prepared for her just moving to Maine. She'd mentioned she was coming for a month, but to just readjust her schedule and to start plans of living in the area full-time had caught him off guard.

She ended the kiss first and pushed herself away from him. He closed his eyes and mentally refocused. "I'm glad you're here," he offered, slowly opening his eyes.

"Are you? Last night, I wasn't so sure."

"Honey, I've never just up and dropped everything and changed my life around."

"Oh, didn't you? When you were eighteen, didn't you accept responsibility for Jess and take her in and care for her, giving up on your own college desires to raise a child?"

"But that's different."

"Okay, then what about the weekend in New York? That was impulsive."

Wayne stepped back and turned away from her.

"Don't walk out on me now, Wayne. We need to talk this through."

"I wasn't leaving. I was just thinking. You're right; it was impulsive. But I'm worried you're giving up too much."

She reached out for his hand and led him to the sofa. "Wayne, there's a lot you don't know about my business. I can sell and resell photographs for years. It's simply being aware of what the market is looking for. I can do that far better from here than traipsing around the world."

"Really?"

"Yes. And there are other things I can do and still earn a salary. Granted, it won't be as plump of a salary as I had been making, but I would still earn a reasonable income. But I've gone a step further. I've started arranging with other photographers to kind of work as their agent, helping them with bookings and scheduling when I'm contacted for a job. And I'd earn a certain percentage of their income for that shoot."

"It's a well-laid-out plan."

"Thanks, but I still don't know where we were headed. Do you?"

"I know what I'd like, but, you're right, we are both rather set in our ways. This month will be quite a test for us."

"Yeah. Except that David and Amber are arriving this weekend with the kids. They're bringing up the rest of my stuff for the master suite."

"And?"

"And they'll probably be staying for a week. The stress has been really hard on them. I might even suggest they leave the kids and go home alone for a week."

Dena's stomach churned loud enough for the entire room to hear it. Thankfully, they were alone.

"I'm going to get you something to eat. We'll talk more when I get back."

"Thanks." She kissed him lightly on the lips. "When I was a kid and fell in love with Bill, I didn't have any fear. I do have serious doubts, Wayne. I've liked being on my own. There's a freedom in it."

"I know. I do understand. When Jess was in college, I found myself enjoying having the house to myself. I missed her, but the house was my own. The 'sound of silence' filled the air. There was a sense of rhythm in the quietness, somehow."

"Exactly. So, can we share our lives with each other?"

"I don't know, Dena. I honestly don't know. I want to, but, as with you, it's a major step."

Dena let out a half chuckle. "*Major* is an understatement."

"Yeah," Wayne sighed. "All right, I'm going now. We'll pick this up when I come back." He tapped her on her knee.

"Okay."

He left the cottage and worked his way back to town. Why was he fighting Dena's move to Maine?

You need help, ol' boy, serious help. Wayne turned into the grocery store parking lot. A few cars were parked next to the building, while a single black sedan in the center of the lot sat under the streetlight. Peter Mayhew, the elderly owner of the store, always parked under that lamp. Precious little happened in the way of crime in this small town, but the precaution had been a wise move.

"Evening, Mr. Mayhew, how are you tonight?" Wayne asked, pulling a red plastic basket from the small pile near the door.

"Fine, fine. Heard that pretty Ms. Russell's back in town. Is that so?"

"Yes, sir. She'll be staying for an entire month. You might have to stock up on some of that fancy city stuff for the lady." Wayne winked.

Peter's bushy white eyebrows rose halfway up his bald head. "Already placed an order. Pastor Russell told me she was coming last week. Any truth to the rumors that you and Ms. Russell are moving in together?"

"Not a word of it. And if you hear anyone speaking such, please let them know Mrs. Russell lives by the same standards Pastor Russell preaches."

"Pleased to hear it. Kids today just don't seem to have the same values."

It was time for Wayne to raise his eyebrows. Dena would love hearing herself referred to as a kid.

"Present company excluded, of course." Peter winked again.

Maybe moving to the city would be a better start for us if we were to get married, he mused.

"What can I get you tonight?" Peter asked.

"Two steaks, sirloin or better, if you have it."

"Delmonico cut?"

"Perfect." Delmonicos were tender, an excellent choice cut from the rib section of the cow.

He picked up a pint of homemade potato salad prepared by Pete's daughter, Mable, and a half dozen ears of corn. He paid for the order, walked outside, and slid the bag over to the passenger side of the truck. *Lord, I just don't want to get in Dena's way. Please give me peace about her decisions regarding her business.*

He pulled out into the street and turned toward the four corners in the center of town. Tires squealed. A black SUV suddenly filled his field of vision and plowed into his left side. Then he saw nothing.

❧

"Mom, there's been an accident."

"What? Who? What happened?" Dena curled the phone cord around her finger. Where was Wayne? He should have been back a half hour ago. Then it dawned on her. "Wayne?"

"I'm afraid so."

"Where is he? Is he okay? What happened?" She reached for her car keys from the counter.

"Some kids were driving too fast and ran the stop sign. The vehicle hit him on the driver's side. He's been hurt, but I don't know how badly. They're driving him up to Ellsworth now. The town doctor couldn't do much for him here, Mom. I drove up to Mayhew's Market just as they were putting him in the ambulance."

"Which hospital? Has Jess been told?"

"No one's called Jess, as far as I know. I was thinking we should wait to hear what the doctors say after they've done some tests."

"I'm going up there. Where is this hospital?"

"In Ellsworth; it's Blue Hill Hospital. I'll take you."

"No, I'll follow you. There's no telling how long I'll be up there."

"All right. Meet me at Mayhew's Market. On second thought, crews may still be cleaning up after the accident." He suggested an alternate meeting place.

"Fine." Dena grabbed her purse and ran out the door. "Oh, Lord, please keep him safe." Tears threatened to fall. *No, I can't. Not yet. I need to drive.* She set her resolve and drove as fast and as cautiously as she could allow herself.

She drove into the market's parking lot about the same time that Jason arrived. He rolled down his window. "Are you all right?"

"I'm fine. How far away is this hospital?"

"An hour and a half. Two hours with traffic."

Dena nodded. She didn't trust herself to speak. She followed Jason down the long, windy roads toward the interstate. "Who cares about schedules?" she asked aloud in the empty car. "We should just get married and follow our hearts. Life is too short. We'll work out the details somehow. Father, heal him and help us so we can be one with You," she prayed, and continued down the highway.

Inside the waiting room, she paced back and forth. Jason had a little pull, since he was clergy, and went back into the ER to discover Wayne slipping in and out of consciousness. He'd also suffered some cracked ribs. They were still checking on internal bleeding, but the doctor was very hopeful.

Dena dialed her home phone in Boston. "Jess?"

"Dena, hi. Did you arrive okay?"

"Fine. Honey, I'm sorry to be the one to tell you this, but your dad's been in an accident. He's okay."

Silence followed, then a sniffle. "Is he all right?"

"He has some broken ribs and he's semiconscious."

"Where is he? How'd it happen? I'm coming up."

"He's in Blue Hill Hospital in Ellsworth. Some kid ran a stop sign by Mayhew's Market and plowed into the driver side door. You're welcome to come up, but there's not much you can do right now. Do me a favor? If you come up, have Trevor come with you. I don't want you driving six hours by yourself with this kind of news."

Jess sniffled again. "All right. Dena, is he really going to be okay?"

"Yes, I haven't seen him yet. The doctor says it looks good. But he'll be sore for quite a while."

"Okay. Can I call you from the road?"

They exchanged numbers, and Dena began calling to ask the rest of the family to be praying, only to discover that Marie already had.

An hour later, Jason was able to go in and visit with Wayne briefly. "He barely knew I was there, Mom. You might as well go home."

"No, I want to see him. I'll wait until I can, then I'll get a room."

"All right. I'll come by sometime tomorrow and bring a change of clothes."

"Thanks, but you don't have to. My overnight bag is still in the backseat of my car."

The night dragged on. By midnight she was allowed to visit Wayne briefly.

She held his hand. Her stomach twisted and churned at the sight of him hooked up to the monitors. "Honey," she whispered and kissed him tenderly on the forehead.

His eyes fluttered open, then closed slowly. "Marry me," he whispered. He opened his eyes again and focused on hers. "Life's too short. We'll work out the schedules. Please say you'll marry me."

She kissed him again and combed his sandy blond hair with her fingers. *Lord, heal him quickly,* she prayed. "Yes, I will. I'll come back in the morning. They won't let me stay more than ten minutes. I love you."

"I love you, too."

❧

Three days later Dena stood in her darkroom and tried to put some order to her files. Amber and David brought up the rest of her files and cabinets. Those had been easy to put in place. But since she'd been living between Boston and Squabbin Bay, she had fallen behind and had a stack of filing to do.

"Mom, I hate to say this, but I think you were taking pictures of the harbor when your mind was somewhere else." Amber handed her the laptop. "I've highlighted the photos in question."

Dena looked at the foggy images. The blurred bow of a boat showed itself to be the focal point. "Ah, those are some of the photos I took while trying to capture a shot of the poachers."

"Poachers?" Amber took the computer back from Dena. "You're going to have to fill me in on that one."

"Amber," David called, "I'm taking the kids to the beach."

"Okay." Amber turned back to her mother. "The house is clear, tell me."

Dena swallowed a light chuckle then filled her daughter in about the poaching. After Wayne's accident, the police had discovered that those same teens had also been responsible for Ben Costa's house fire. Ben himself had been responsible for his boat blowing up. He'd left the gas on and a cigar still burning on the edge of his sink. But that still hadn't solved the issue of the poachers.

"Wow, and I thought your life would be too boring up here. Do you think life might be calmer in Boston?"

Dena chuckled. "You know, it might be." She reached for the photographs of Chad's wedding. "Can you sort these and place them in order? Thankfully, I made doubles and sent them to the kids so they could order the ones they want enlarged."

"Sure."

Dena opened another box and lifted out the series of negatives and contact prints from the Colorado white-water rafting trip. She labeled the file folder and placed all negatives and CDs from the trip in the folder.

"Dena," Wayne called from someplace inside the house.

"I'm in the darkroom." She got up and met him at the doorway. "Hey, what's up? How are you feeling?"

"Okay. I'm still sore, but my head isn't throbbing anymore. I hate to do this, but my dad is insisting that I spend the evening with him, something about his retirement plan. I'm sorry, but I won't be able to have dinner with you and the kids tonight."

"No problem. I've yet to meet your father."

Wayne reached over and put his hands on her waist. "You will. He's a good man but has gotten very self-centered since he retired."

"Hi, Wayne." Amber walked up from behind Dena. "Mom, these were in Chad's wedding pictures. I think they need to be filed with those other pictures of the poachers."

"You got pictures?"

"No. Well, nothing that shows who it is or even if it is the poachers."

"These are clear," Amber offered.

"They can't be the poachers. I took those before Chad's wedding."

Wayne reached for them. "May I see?"

"Sure." Amber handed over the half dozen photographs.

Dena looked over Wayne's shoulder. His hands started to shake. "When did you take these?"

"The week after the carnival, back in early May."

He let the photographs fall. "I have to go. That's my father." Wayne slowly stomped out of the house.

Dena picked the photographs up off the floor. *His father?*

epilogue

Three months later

Dena straightened her dress and looked in the mirror. The past three months had been difficult. Dena's photographs caught Wayne's father as the poacher. Apparently, he'd gotten into gambling and lost all of his savings and then some. She smiled at her reflection. Wayne's desire to help his parents had left him destitute. Wayne had sold his house and used his savings to pay off his father's gambling debts, along with the sale of his parents' home in Squabbin Bay. Dena had grown to love Wayne even more as they worked through the situation together.

"Ready, Mom?" Amber poked her head around the door.

"Ready."

The organ music floated into the room. She'd been in this room before, primping Brianne for her wedding to Chad. Now, she was doing the same for herself.

"Hey, Mom." Jess stopped short. She'd been calling Dena "Mom" for a couple of months now—ever since moving in after Wayne sold the house and moved onto his boat. "Wow, you look great. Dad's going to flip when he sees you."

Dena chuckled. "I hope not. I don't want to see the inside of the hospital again for a mighty long time." She turned to her new daughter. "How is he?"

"Better. Grandpa and Grandma are here. Grandpa is still a bit touchy about Dad having paid off his debts. Grandma is so grateful they didn't lose their condo in Florida. But I can't wait until the two of you tie the knot. I need some relief."

Dena laughed. Jess had moved back to Maine shortly

167

after the accident. The dream job in Boston was simply that, a dream. Nothing in the office ran smoothly, the other employees didn't work well together, and everyone was out to move themselves ahead and not help anyone else. Jess's relationship with Trevor was cooling off. He wasn't interested in living in Maine, and, in fact, he had little motivation about doing anything more than was required of him. He was a good person, but Jess found him lacking in more and more areas once they were apart and she was no longer looking at him through her emotions. Dena fired off another prayer for Jess's future husband. He was out there, Dena knew, but she was glad Jessica wasn't too broken up about the end of her relationship with Trevor.

"Wow!" Amber came in with Dena's bouquet. "You look great, Mom."

"Thanks."

She and Wayne had decided on a simple wedding with no attendants. If they had allowed one of their children to stand in, they'd have to have all of them, so it had been simpler to have none.

"It's time." Marie smiled. "Are you ready, Mom?"

The fears had washed away the night of the accident. "Oh, yeah. We'd have been married a month or two ago if—"

The room erupted in laughter.

"Right, if you two ever stopped long enough to stop worrying about each other's careers. Face it, the accident was a blessing." Brianne stood with her hands on her hips, her six-month belly protruding.

Again the room erupted into laughter. "I think we could have gotten there without the accident. After all, we could have married sooner if Wayne wasn't so stubborn about. . Never mind."

"I think he was more concerned about carrying you over the threshold," Jess offered.

Dena's eyes widened. "He wouldn't dare."

Jess laughed.

Marie took charge and encouraged everyone to take their seats in the sanctuary. Dena took a moment. Closing her eyes, she sighed and released the last of her fears over to the Lord. With total confidence, she stepped out of the small room, headed toward the center aisle, and paused. Marie signaled the organist.

The music changed to the traditional wedding march.

Her smile broadened. She took a step and rounded the corner. She caught a glimpse of Wayne's sparkling green eyes. Her heart fluttered. *Dear Lord, I do love those green eyes. But more importantly, I love the man who knows how to wear 'em.*

ૐ

Wayne shifted his stance upon seeing Dena walk down the aisle. He locked his gaze on hers, and they stayed focused on one another. *Thank You, Lord.*

Jason began the service. Wayne held Dena's silky hands. He couldn't believe this incredible woman wanted him above all others.

"In sickness and health," Jason said.

Wayne and Dena winked at one another.

At some point he and she said the appropriate "I do's."

"You may kiss the bride." Wayne leaned in and kissed her warm lips, then closed the distance between himself and his bride and held her, not wanting to let her go.

Reluctantly, they pulled apart. Jason concluded. "I now have the honor of presenting to you Mr. and Mrs. Wayne Kearns."

The congregation stood and clapped.

"I love you," Wayne whispered.

"I love you, too."

"So where are you taking me for our honeymoon?" Wayne wiggled his eyebrows and led her down the aisle.

She'd kept it a secret. With all the family troubles and his healing from the accident, she felt she could at least ease his burden by planning the honeymoon.

"Hawaii."

"I'm going to love being married to you. Will we be on a photo op?"

Dena giggled. "You never know."

A Letter To Our Readers

Dear Reader:

In order that we might better contribute to your reading enjoyment, we would appreciate your taking a few minutes to respond to the following questions. We welcome your comments and read each form and letter we receive. When completed, please return to the following:

Fiction Editor
Heartsong Presents
PO Box 719
Uhrichsville, Ohio 44683

1. Did you enjoy reading *Photo Op* by Lynn A. Coleman?
   ❏ Very much! I would like to see more books by this author!
   ❏ Moderately. I would have enjoyed it more if

   _____

   _____

   _____

2. Are you a member of **Heartsong Presents**? ❏ Yes ❏ No
   If no, where did you purchase this book? _____

   _____

3. How would you rate, on a scale from 1 (poor) to 5 (superior), the cover design? _____

4. On a scale from 1 (poor) to 10 (superior), please rate the following elements.

   ____ Heroine   ____ Plot
   ____ Hero   ____ Inspirational theme
   ____ Setting   ____ Secondary characters

5. These characters were special because? _____

_____

_____

6. How has this book inspired your life? _____

_____

_____

7. What settings would you like to see covered in future
   Heartsong Presents books? _____

_____

_____

8. What are some inspirational themes you would like to see
   treated in future books? _____

_____

_____

9. Would you be interested in reading other **Heartsong
   Presents** titles? ❑ Yes ❑ No

10. Please check your age range:
    ❑ Under 18   ❑ 18-24
    ❑ 25-34   ❑ 35-45
    ❑ 46-55   ❑ Over 55

Name _____

Occupation _____

Address _____

City, State, Zip_____

RHODE ISLAND
Weddings

3 stories in 1

Join three Rhode Island
couples as they work to
strengthen their love in
the midst of personal trials.

Contemporary, paperback, 352 pages, 5³/₁₆" x 8 "

Please send me _____ copies of *Rhode Island Weddings*.
I am enclosing $6.97 for each.
(Please add $3.00 to cover postage and handling per order. OH add 7% tax.
If outside the U.S. please call 740-922-7280 for shipping charges.)

Name_____

Address _____

City, State, Zip _____

To place a credit card order, call 1-740-922-7280.
Send to: Heartsong Presents Readers' Service, PO Box 721, Uhrichsville, OH 44683